Love Matters

Herman Edel

Copyright © 2018 Herman Edel

Love Matters

Applegate Valley Publishing
www.applegatevalleypublishing.com

Contact: edelhermedel@gmail.com
or info@applegatevalleypublishing.com

Design by Deborah Perdue, Illumination Graphics
www.illuminationgraphics.com

Paperback: ISBN-13: 978-0-9983677-1-2

Introduction

*I*n the previous novels I have written, I always had in mind the title of the book I was about to write. This time I started scribbling away without a clue as to the title. It was the constant offerings of friends that finally brought forth "Love Matters." Those words opened the path for the entire book.

My dear friend and advisor, John Baxter, brought me to that ultra-talented craftsman Bruce Bayard who taught me how to get the most out of very old photos.

If you are as angered by the photo on page 202 as I was, I heartily suggest you visit the Southern Oregon Historical Society for many more of same.

Jim Amberg, my Shakespeare consultant, led me down a very difficult path and how to understand Shakespeare.

Joy Dickson and Scott Kaiser introduced me to the wonders of the Oregon Shakespeare Festival and the brilliant actors and actresses who illuminate the three stages they perform on.

That incredible photographer, Charles Ericson, gave me the use of a wonderful picture you will see in the book.

Barbara Tricarico, a wondrous writer and photographer, was a most encouraging voice of help.

My wife, Mardie, time after time, unearthed ghastly errors in this book. Much of 'Love Matters' came from her advice on what I was creating in this book. I thank her and all the others on this page for making this task an easy and exciting trip.

Chapter One

*B*en Dawson and Edith Simpson first met in Miller's Pig Sty, which could not have been a more appropriate name for this pitiful bar. Being situated in the small town of Hopewell, Virginia, it attracted a crowd of deadbeats looking for cheap booze.

It survived by being but a few miles south of the far more prosperous Richmond, Virginia. The bar catered to a class of clients from either city who preferred the low cost for either a beer or a shot of cheap booze.

Ben spotted Edith the moment he opened the rather tarnished front door. As he sauntered over to her, he knew she would be easy meat.

Edith had gotten to the bar early that evening and was deep into her sixth straight of the bar's cheapest booze. She was far gone when Ben first approached her with his always successful words.

"What's a beautiful woman like you doing alone in this dive?"

He followed up with the very suave comment, "What say, good looking, can an ugly old guy like me be buying a beautiful gal like you anything she wants?"

Seeing as she had been drinking for over an hour and was running short of change, those two words were music to her ears. She managed to bring up just one legible reply.

"In my mind, yes sir, in my mind any man willing to put a Scotch and Soda down in front of me hain't nothin but a real fine man that I know I will like.

To their mutual delight, they quickly discovered that both their families had migrated to America from Belgium. Since they had different last names, it never dawned on either one that they still might have come from the same family line.

It took less than thirty seconds for the desired drink to appear in front of Edith as Ben had ordered it for her the moment he entered the bar and spotted this available female forlornly seated at the bar with an empty glass in her hand.

She lifted the glass in a toast to her new friend, as he nodded his head in acknowledgement that this was to be his bed mate for later that night. It didn't take much smooth talk for him to waltz her out of the bar and into the dingy hotel that was just around the corner.

Of course, first comes first and that meant many a Scotch was enjoyed before they could get down to the serious activities of the evening. Prior to heading to the dingy hotel, their conversation seemed to dwindle away as words were not of much importance.

Of greater import was how quickly the Scotch told them that it was perfectly fine to tumble out of Miller's back door. One passionate kiss led them to start to strip off each other's clothes as they walked towards the hotel. The dampness of the grass led them a bit faster to the comforts of the hotel.

Once in their room, they spent a pleasant few minutes imbibing and toying with one another, but the more important evening's activity soon reared its head and these two animals were soon tearing at one another. Niceties were not on the agenda for these two. Sleep occasionally gave them pause in their wars upon one another, but finally all their lusts seemed to be satisfied, and a drunken sleep brought peace to them.

They both woke up the next morning absolutely naked and practically atop one another. She didn't particularly like the sight of him, and he thought she absolutely stunk like rotten food.

Why they started seeing one another on a regular basis was beyond all. First they would get as drunk as feasible. Then they would retire for hours of crazed sex. The next morning they would wake up hating one another.

They both soon realized that their coupling was due to the fact that no one else in the bar would spend any time with them. The fact of the matter is that Louie G., the owner of Miller's, would on most nights toss them both out of his pub.

Three months later Edith, unhappily, discovered that she was in dire trouble. She was pregnant. She insisted that the father had to be Ben, since she had not slept with anyone since that crazy first night.

He fought that decision, claiming that he was sterile, or that he had used a condom every night, or that he had never had an orgasm with her.

She ended all discussion as to who was the father when she introduced her brother Charlie to Ben. Charlie was six foot three and weighed two hundred and fifty pounds. When Charlie told Ben of how much he enjoyed beating the crap out of little guys and then showed Ben his favorite hand gun, all arguments disappeared.

The rationale for their marriage emerged with the birth of Catherine just short of a year after that first meeting. Like her mother, Edith, the girl grew up to be a querulous and quarrelsome child. She was as unattractive as her mother and as dull as her father.

Catherine's parents, neither too bright, did not have a clue about raising a child nor did they care to learn about it. Ben had somehow graduated from high school, while Edith left her high school in her junior year.

Ben and Edith continued frequenting Miller's where they did little talking to one another. She concentrated on the consumption of as many shots as she could handle. He was the happiest when he could corral a female at the bar and tell her about the troubles their wonderful city had survived.

"Why in 1950 over 184 people contracted that Infantile Paralysis, and over 17 people died from that damned disease when it hit this town. The only good thing we did was if one of the town's blacks got the disease, we wouldn't let them into our hospital but made them go to Richmond to get hospital help."

That invariably brought forth a chuckle, to which the following was always added.

"The greatest kick we have ever had in this town was not many years ago. On December 23, 2001, Warren Taylor, a local fool, rode his wheel chair into the Wytheville post office and threatened to blow it up. He then took three hostages by leveling his gun at them. Finally, one of the policemen talked him out of his craziness. They found he only had a crazy mouth, a 45, and no bullets."

One night Edith decided she would go out for some fresh air. She declaimed to Ben that she would be back in about fifteen minutes. He in turn just nodded his head knowing that his dear wife was out to get a new piece of tail.

Not fifteen minutes later the crowd at Miller's heard fierce screaming. Several of the more aggressive men at the bar burst out to see what it was all about. They returned shortly with a much beaten Edith. No one knew who the two men were that she said had attacked her as she was about to enter the bar.

More importantly, no one knew that the young men were identical twin brothers nor did they learn anything pertinent about them.

What would have deeply bothered the customers of Miller's was the fact that the two men who had attacked Edith were pledgees of a fraternity from a nearby college. Their drunken assignment was to have sex with the first women they met. Some ten senior members of the fraternity had observed their successful intercourse and were more than delighted with their pledges success at their assignment.

What particularly bothered Edith was that she never knew who the culprits were that had raped her. Smilingly she did confess to herself that no matter who they had been, they were one of the best bed partners she had ever had.

Shortly thereafter Edith became pregnant again. With Edith's loose attention to her bed partners no one had a clue as to who the father was. Every man who even slightly knew Edith had vowed never to sleep with that 'witch' again and that included Ben. All staunchly adhered to that vow.

Common talk at Miller's suggested that Ben had tried to kill his wife at least several times. He had finally tired of her being known as the local slut who would sleep around with any man who was in dire need for any sort of a lay

The following night he appeared at the bar where several of his fellow drinkers noticed several scruff marks on his face. They judged him guilty of losing the previous night's activity, though Edith looked a lot worse than Ben.

It did her no good when she discovered to her horror that she was pregnant again and she was growing at an awesome rate. A stop at the local hospital revealed the unwelcome news that she would be delivering two babies erelong.

Ben stayed away from Miller's for some time thereafter.

The two new children's births was accompanied with a full catalogue of curse words from Ben and Edith. They never stopped blaming the one boy and one girl for ruining their life. Their total distaste for the children never varied.

Equally persistent was everyone's wondering about who could have been the father of these two wunderkinds. Certainly it could not have been Ben, for the boy was obviously quite handsome and showed signs of much intelligence. Edith had named him Richard and common talk tried to locate a Richard who was crazy enough to bed down with Edith. It was just Edith's favorite name. The little girl was never formally named.

Both the boy and the girl were simply ignored by their supposed parents who did not care one wit about whether they would live or die.

Unfortunately, the little girl remained quite small which added to the distaste Ben had for her. Ben found nothing to like about this wee child that he called 'Miss Nothing.' One morning after almost a whole night of her crying, Ben rose and plucked her from the crib she shared with her brother. He pushed the boy to the side of the crib and wrapped the girl in a blanket.

Stealthily, he crept out of the house. Within minutes he met up with a young woman who had just recently lost her baby to a serious case of pneumonia. Within moments the baby was exchanged for a twenty dollar bill given to him by a very drunk young girl.

No matter how badly he was treated the little boy grew rapidly and nothing could wipe the smile from his face. Ethel enjoyed the boy while Ben was not allowed to even so much as touch the lad.

Little Richard was, even at the earliest of ages, far sharper than his oafish father. Soon Richard said and did whatever he wanted to. They allowed the boy complete freedom and with his exercise, it became apparent that the real adult was the sober young baby and not the drunken adults.

What had been most harmful for Richard was watching his parents tear at one another in pursuing their ever demanding sexual adventures. They did what they wanted to do with the boy watching all. Even at his very early age, their every action disgusted him.

Since Ben never had enough cash for even the mangiest of hookers and Edith's horrid reputation had left the horniest of old men disdainful of sex with 'that crazy broad,' she and Ben returned to each other as their only means of sexual satisfaction. It was far from a love affair but it somehow answered the loveless craving that was their sole motivation.

Each maintained their hatred for one another, but nonetheless screamed through their passions.

As Richard grew, so did his hatred of these people who claimed to be his parents. Their lack of restraint and their constantly tearing at one another was sickening to him even through his youngest years. To them anything was fair if it brought them some sort of sexual satisfaction. If this was what was gratifying, then Rich didn't want to have any part of it.

In his early days at school he once asked a teacher about the disgusting habits of his parents. In detail he told of the sexual adventures they put on display for him and Catherine.

The very wise teacher weakly responded, "Well maybe they are far sicker than we believe them to be."

That answer left Richard even more appalled. He knew that his parents hated each other. They hardly spoke to each other, and when they did so, it was as if they were snarling at one another.

Ever persistent in his efforts to teach Rich the joys of sex, Ben launched a new campaign.

"You know you'll soon be dying to get a piece of ass. Why don't you start with your sister Catherine – she's ripe for the plucking."

Rich looked at his farther and spit out, "Leave me alone you sick bastard."

It was the first time he had ever used the word. He did not know what it meant only that it infuriated Ben.

In response Ben instantly labeled Rich as a homosexual.

Chapter Two

Not having a clue as to what that word 'homosexual' meant didn't bother Rich one bit. Nevertheless, he did go the school library where they had huge dictionaries. He had just turned eight and, as the smartest kid in his grade, it was important for him to know what his father thought he was.

The definition was rather simple. Homosexual was defined as 'relating to ones having sexual attraction for members of one's own sex.' The words 'gay' or 'lesbian' further confused him. No matter how he studied those words he was not in the least bit enlightened by the definitions.

Rich was amazed that Ben knew such a long word. He rationalized that if it came from Ben, it could not be worth using and therefore he would never use it. Since he did not know anybody who called himself a 'homosexual,' Rich silently vowed forthwith that sex between a man and a woman meant he could indulge in that. The only problem he had with that decision was that Ben and Edith's activities disgusted him so much that he could not think of himself doing anything as horrific as what they did.

His distaste for both his parents led to his almost total avoidance of either of them. Anything they told him to do, he pointedly ignored. Ben kept up his campaign of trying to control Rich but Edith hardly ever spoke to him. Accordingly, Edith all but disappeared from his life. It became a constant battle to pull further and further away from both Ben and Edith.

Rich would ignore his father's constant pressure by claiming to be sick or had too much home work to do or, when he really wanted to bother Ben, he blatantly lied to him claiming to have been doing it with several girls in his class.

"Anyway, it's not such a big deal, and I really didn't enjoy it so much."

Ben knew that Rich was lying and finally gave up. "That damn son of mine must be a homo. How could he turn down getting laid if he wasn't a homo?"

This failure particularly pleased Edith. Anything that harmed Ben was a delight to her. She further enjoyed the times when Ben was away from home, and she had the freedom to bring in any bum who was in need of a free hour with her. As with Ben, her sexual hunger with said lover was placed on full view to her children.

Ben and Edith did have a few friends who would bet anything that young Richard could not have been sired by Ben. The boy looked like neither of his parents and was more affable and far more intelligent than his sister who had preceded him.

Richard was obviously bright, and all his teachers acclaimed his abilities in school and how gracious he was to all around him. No matter his values, Richard received no favors from his family.

His parents abhorred him, and his sister did all she could to plague him every moment they had to spend together.

Rich was just eight years old when a tiny boy, named Timothy by Edith, was born to her. This was her fourth child and in all truth, neither Ben nor Edith knew who the male parent really was.

From the very first they knew that there was something drastically wrong with this child. He just lay there all the day long, hardly moving. His eyes were almost perpetually closed, and the only sounds that came from the child were more like howls than the cries of a young baby. As he grew older all knew that this was one very sick little boy. Ben was certain he was not the father, while Edith did not have a care as to who the father was.

They both were as wanton as they had ever been. Edith had gone back to her taking on anyone who could provide an erection, and Ben had never changed from lusting for anything called a female. On occasion they had a fling with one another but there was neither love nor delight in their use of one another. The relationship between parents and children worsened with each passing day. They rarely spoke to their daughter, gave little heed to Richard, their second child, and totally ignored Tim their newest.

Timothy was a puzzle to both Edith and Ben. Catherine hated this strange new member of the family and never so much as looked at the boy while Ben gave no credence to its existence.

Rich was the only one who acknowledged the birth of this little boy. He spent the bulk of his free time at the side of the brother he had immediately fallen in love with.

Rich would feed the baby, knowing that none of the others in this hellish family would pay any attention to the tiny boy. He would wash his brother and constantly whisper silly words which put a smile on the baby's face. He would constantly talk to this speechless little thing..

He kept telling his little brother that laughing and smiling was the only way to go, while knowing full well that the only thing that reached the little thing was when he was tickled. Rich was the only one in the family who gave a thought to the obviously ailing baby. He treated Tim with kindness and, in return, fully believed that the little one knew and liked him.

Richard had fallen in love with his little brother from the first, and the little boy seemed to share that feeling as well. Rich spent his every spare moment with little Timmy. He loved to tickle the boy and make funny faces at him so that the two of them could laugh at each other. Rich firmly believed that little Tim knew who his older brother was.

Though they cared little for the two oldest of their children, Ben and Edith had no feelings at all for Tim. Since they now very rarely had sex with each other they attributed this birth to some God given mistake.

Ben's sole remark about his latest child was "That Timothy will be the death of us. He is a damned ignoramus."

Amazingly the boy, with Rich's help, learned to speak. Both of the boys grew excited when Tim understood new words. They would laugh when Timothy would squeak out a word that Rich had just taught his younger brother.

A wonderful love grew between the wise young man and the unknowing waif. Their bonds grew with each moment that they spent together. Oddly enough Rich received an ever growing delight from watching Tim's growth while Tim just accepted that Rich was his best friend who would always be there for him.

Rich received great pleasure when he treated his little brother to a special gift on his sixth birthday. The gift, a package of some twenty colorful little marbles, brought an instant smile to blossom all over Tim's face. The little boy fondled each of the marbles before he looked up to Rich and haltingly said, "Rich you are my best friend, and I will always love you."

Chapter Three

$\mathcal{R}$ich had two pleasures in his life. The first was getting Tim to smile and the second was the friendship that developed between himself and a young English teacher, Bill Kaplan, who also was the director of all the school plays.

They first met when Rich was twelve and the brightest student in the teacher's class. Kaplan and Rich found an intellectual bonding that went far beyond the classroom. Kaplan's wife and their six year old daughter opened two worlds for Rich, the wonders that were hidden in theatre and the glories of intellectual stimulation, both presented in a loving home relationship.

The teacher found a rare thing in Rich; a young man who was eager to learn, while the young student found a teacher who graciously accepted wisdom from the mouth of a young student. This strange bonding of two very bright young people with a vast difference in age grew as the boy would often have dinner with the teacher and his wife and child. It didn't take too long before each night Tim became the fourth diner at this, for him, wondrous meal.

What brought them together was that Rich and his teacher friend had discovered a common love – the theatre. The teacher was a fine director, who found great pleasure in directing his students in at least three plays each year, and it was apparent that Rich was as much in love with theatre as was his friend and teacher.

By the time Rich was fourteen years old, great theatrical activity was found in Roanoke, a big city not too far off – there Rich would, every now and then, find a small part in a play that Kaplan would direct.

Their trips back and forth from Roanoke were a brilliant opportunity for Rich to learn everything his teacher could bring to him, while Kaplan enjoyed spending a great deal of time lecturing Rich about what a good actor does.

Kaplan's favorite tenet was, "When you step out on stage, you can't be just acting out a character. You must be that character."

Due to those ever constant lectures, Rich knew more about the art of acting than most of the performers on Broadway.

As Rich grew older, he knew he was not homosexual but memories of his parent's sexual activities kept him away from the normal boy-girl games. He was a total loner.

His parents treated him as if he were the enemy in their household.

Edith's favorite quote about her son was "That boy seems to be forever at war with us. He loves artsy-fartsy things. We are sure he is a homosexual, and the hell with him for that."

Tim's one delight was that Rich seemed to be always at his side. For Rich, his little brother was a constant joy. At times Tim could be angry at the world but with a tickle or a laugh Rich could always calm him down.

His parents aging did not change their wanton way of life, but did alter some of their more outrageous ways of life. They cared not that their eldest child, Catherine, had long since dropped out of school and run off with boys she just met.

Not too long afterwards Catherine reappeared at their doorstep. She was allowed to stay at the house because she had a small job at the local supermarket and was constantly stealing food and other valuable items for use at their home.

Ben had thoughts again of bedding her but the first time he made a pass at her she beat him off with a heavy hammer that was her favorite possession. She was quite clear in telling them that she was here just to have a place to sleep and, as she quaintly said, "Just stay the fuck away from me."

Timothy was just six when they began to drop him off at their local church early each Sunday morning. In truth this was more for their benefit than the boy's. To be apart from Tim was a joy to his parents.

It was not too long afterwards that Rich was delegated with that duty. Edna kept explaining to him that in church he and Tim would learn how to be good and not to be bad. Oddly enough, Timothy enjoyed church very much. Much of his liking of the church came about because he loved all the music he heard there.

At times he would get bored with the repetitive nature of the service and he would let all the congregants know that he was bored with the service.

It was up to Rich to calm Tim down so that he didn't disrupt all in the church. But at times the outburst would last far too long, while at others, it was here and gone in but minutes. Though they tried hard enough, neither Richard nor his parents could determine what set Tim off.

Rich worried himself silly but never could discover what the impetus was that would drive his usually sweet and pleasant little brother into what seemed to be an evil being.

He was obviously mentally incompetent. His reading abilities were quite limited. He had an explosive temper that would burst forth with no explanation about what caused the outbreak. Yet, moments later, he might be as quiet and sweet a little boy as one could be.

Friends, neighbors and local tradesmen learned to follow the path taken by the parents of Timothy. They too ignored the cute little boy who just garbled his words. Truth be told, they were a bit frightened of this sickly looking little boy.

Ben's favorite quote about the boy was either. "Don't say a word to the little dummy. He'll never understand anything you say, and sure as hell you won't understand what he is burbling out to you."

His favorite comment to Tim was, "Just keep that stupid yap of yours closed."

The boy learned only one thing. His brother, Richard, made him happy and Tim adored him. By the time Tim turned five, he only recognized Rich as someone he could turn to. Rich talked to him and slowly started to teach Tim how to read. Tim began to put together words and their meanings. A wonderful smile began to appear when letters formed into words and began to mean something.

Though he was far from a good reader, and the words were often far from accurate in meaning, he delighted in this new sport called reading. Bad as it was, he boasted about his ability to read and was quick to tell everyone that Rich had taught him to be a perfect reader. Prior to his eighth birthday, Tim might be considered an awkward, shy boy. Yes he was shy and slow, but he still loved to run and jump and scream out to the world about everything he did. If Rich was there all, was good, but all collapsed when Rich was away. The outbursts lessened to some degree as Tim grew older but the threat of it was always present.

Throughout his life, Tim remained a puzzle. At times, particularly when he was alone with Rich, he was sweet and tender, but it was only when he was with Rich. With others, one never knew which Tim would appear.

Chapter Four

Neither of the parents had permanent employment. Ben would hire on as a field hand at one or another farm. Edith had part time work cleaning up at several local groceries. Very few people conversed with them, for most people considered them little more than 'White Trash.' To say that they were indigent was an insult to the word. They were the laziest of workers and keeping a job for any period of time was beyond their capabilities.

The one legitimate tie between the two was that both were offspring of folks who had come from Belgium to America shortly after 1913.

Each had come from a somewhat famed Belgian family named Annenberg Buchholz. Their heritage claimed a small fortune made from a successful farming business.

One small wing of the family decided to migrate to the United States. They were shortly thereafter followed by yet another Annenberg family. Oddly enough, neither family looked to try to make strong ties with the others of their family.

It was traditional for emigrant families newly arriving in America to search out their fellow countrymen. Not this group. Here there was no joining of hands to produce a strong family tie. Instead, animosities that had thrived in the old country, grew fiercely in this foreign land.

The eruption of World War One enhanced an odd situation. Those who stayed on the farms in the old county grew wealthier and, willingly, sent funds to their American counterparts who were having a troubled financial time. But as the war intensified, so did old country hatred of one family for the other.

Those in Europe had to produce more food and yet received lesser payment for same. Those in America fell deeper and deeper in debt and could not understand why their Belgian family's had significantly cut the funds they were sending to those in America

Actually, many of their Belgium neighbors survived the troubled early days in America, while slowly but surely becoming typical refugees fighting their way up the working class. But the heritage of Ben and Edith Morton left them hating, rather than loving even one another.

Of occasion, they might enjoy the rare sexual encounter with a stranger that pleased them, but even there that encounter was rarely repeated. They only cried out at the cruel world that had left them together, but poor as can be and with a mate they detested, and apart from the rest of the more fortunate world.

The world had deserted them and the Morton's replied in kind.

Cheating and stealing was considered a viable manner of progressing by the likes of the Morton's. Their children were not in any way appreciated by their parents, who felt them to be mere obstacles in the way of their enjoyment of life. All they were taught was that life is a bitch and you've got to fight every inch of the way through this life of theirs

Sexual activity was the only activity that pleased them. Living together was a mere convenience. Sex was purely a moment of hysteria to be enjoyed by one or the other. Rarely was it for mutual pleasure.

Edith preferred dalliances with new found chaps from Miller's, while Ben, in turn, enjoyed the wham bam that he indulged in. He found the exchange of buying an orgasm from a hooker and the freedom for him to do whatever he wanted with them was more to his liking.

Rich, their first male child, was the complete antithesis of his sister. From the earliest, he knew that he was not meant to be a part of this so called family. He knew that he must rear himself apart from these people he lived with. His one goal in life was to get away from these horrors who claimed he was their child. He was like a foreigner who had been stranded in an adverse world from which he must as soon as possible escape.

The arrival of Tim, whom Rich had immediately fallen in love with, forced him to delay his departure from the daily torture he suffered.

Instead he concentrated on learning and was, by far, the brightest student in his school. He also discovered what his career would be when he was given the lead role in a class play. He would be, no, he must be an actor in the world that awaited him.

His first professional acting role earned him a minimal fee but he relished in the fact that he was being paid at all. He was cast in a tiny role in a small play that was presented by a touring New York company. All the lead roles were taken by New York actors, but there were a few small roles available for locals. Rich was commended by the producer who told him in the strongest tones, "Get your ass up to New York. You have the goods to make it there."

While still in high school, Rich worked at a myriad of part-time jobs – the local library, the corner drug store or any other premise that would offer any pay. The money thus earned was meticulously placed in the bank situated on the closest corner. Those funds were never touched. Obviously, not a word of this was ever mentioned to his parents.

His firmest rule was, yes, you can save, but, no, you cannot touch any of it until you are ready to move out of this hell you now occupy. This allowed him to earn and save as much money as he could.

Word of Rich's skills had been passed down from each touring show that came to Rich's little town. His little bank account grew each year, permitting him to advance his theatre skills and in doing so, build his savings account. It took a year of being the ultimate scrooge to acquire enough money before he could afford to take flight from the horror he now lived in and see if he could survive in New York City.

Mournful tears flowed from Timothy when he learned that his only friend would be leaving him.

"Rich please don't leave me?"

"Believe me I'll have you up in New York with me as soon as I can. You are going to love it there, and I'll be visiting you as often as I can while we are apart."

Tim turned away from his brother with tears flowing down his face. A strange feeling crept over him. He couldn't put anything into words and nothing made sense to him. He didn't know why but he didn't care if he died right then and there. He managed to grab a blanket and throw it over his head, as he crawled under his bed.

He was a totally lost ten-year old who didn't understand what was happening to him. An empty feeling came over him.

What he did not understand was that he was suffering his first depression. Through the remainder of his life he would periodically face a time when sadness would overcome him. Fighting it off took him to crawling under a bed or hiding beneath a chair, or flying out of the house and burying himself under a big tree.

That was Tim at his very worst. It was to happen many, many times throughout his life. When happy, he was a joy to behold, but all too often, he was stricken by a depression that would overwhelm him. Then he brought grief to all.

No one had ever bothered to take Tim to a doctor who could puzzle out Tim's problems.

Rich, on his own, had read of two diseases that might lay claim to Tim. One was Autism, and a more recently discovered disease, named Asperger's. Both laid claim to all the problems that at one time or another laid claim to Tim.

There was no doctor where they lived who had the faintest claim to any knowledge of either disease.

The tears that flowed down his younger brother's face shouted out forcibly to Rich. One night he approached his parents with his plan to soon take his young brother with him to New York.

"He is always happy when he is with me and never finds room for a smile when he is with you."

It did not take Ben and Edith long to realize that they would be better off without their two major problems.

"You want to take that piece of garbage with you, then fine. But don't expect us to welcome either of you home ever again."

True to his word, that day came soon afterwards. Without a word he was gone. The next Saturday he came back to his old home. He took a room at a nearby small YMCA and then stole Tim out of their house and spent the weekend with him in a small room that they both loved.

The only time that a smile appeared on Tim's face was when Rich stole Tim from his old home. The saddest days were when he had to return to his parents rooms.

"I'll be back every Saturday and spend the weekend with you, until the time comes when I can bring you up to New York to live with me."

Those words left Tim with a face full of smiles that stayed with him from Monday to Friday, knowing that Rich would appear on the following day.

Chapter Five

Timothy often recalled the days some years ago when he arrived at school age. He had been told by Rich that it might be a little trying at first, but if he played it cool, he could get to like school.

Rich was way off target. Tim was tormented by his fellow students from the first moment he entered the school building. And that was relatively easy as compared to his entrance into the place called a classroom. Which, in his mind, should have been called a prison ward.

The fact of the matter was that he would never have been sent to school but that his mother found the school to be a perfect spot to dump her idiot child for four hours each morning.

With great remorse, he remembered how sad he had been as he sat alone each day watching each of his classmates enjoy themselves. He hadn't a clue about what he was supposed to do.

Schooling brought Tim face to face with his second major depression. He didn't know why but he was terribly frightened by all the frenetic activity going on around him. Typically for Tim, when he got frightened he grew sad. He spent most of that first day fighting off the tears that sadness brought to him.

By the time his mother came for him, which was a full hour later than all the other kindergarteners had been picked up, he was a basket case.

It was as if silence and sadness were the sole roles he could handle. After much supplication from his teachers and the Principal, who claimed he didn't belong in school, Ben and Edith finally agreed to give Tim yet another year out of school but he did not last through the first few months of the year.

His parents were given all sorts of alternatives to formal schooling but since all this horror still came with costs to pay for same they ignored keeping him in school.

Ben's answer to the problem was simple enough

"That damned kid is as dumb as a dead pig. It's stupid to waste money that we don't have trying to educate him. He's not ever going to wake up and be ready to go back to school, and we can't afford paying for some phony-baloney teacher to waste their time with him. If he ever wakes up, then we'll worry about it."

Richard immediately became Tim's personal tutor. Each time on his visit to his brother he would bring a new book for them to read and to study. Of most importance was that Tim, under Rich's tutelage, understood the meanings of all the words in the books though he never mastered the art of spelling.

Somehow Rich found that simple arithmetic was something that Tim liked. It was also easy for Rich to make learning math a fun activity for Tim. As Tim grew older, he became a veritable wiz at handling numbers.

Rich also accepted the fact that he and his brother would always be different. Yes, progress was made, and their conversations became meaningful, as Tim even began to have talks with just about anyone willing to take the time to talk to him. As sweet as he was, he even tried talking to his sister and his parents. Their response to him was less than minimal.

Rich kept shouting to all that, behind Tim's frailties, lay a brain that someday would emerge.

Both boys were totally attached to each other. Rich would spew out to Timothy his dreams about how he, Richard Morton, would someday become a famed actor.

"And when I do you will be right at my side cheering me on."

On his own, Tim wondered why his parents always screamed constantly at Rich calling him a 'gay bastard.' He had no idea about what that meant, but it sure must be something terrible, for when they screamed those words, Rich would turn white with anger.

It was on one trip home from New York that Rich was surprised on entering the old apartment that there was not a bit of noise to be heard. Normally, his sister would be playing the radio at some outrageously loud volume; his parents would be screaming at one another and Tim, on a good day, would be jumping from chair to chair and room to room.

Finally Rich heard what seemed to be whimpering coming out of what once had been his and Timothy's room. He pushed open the door and again heard the muffled sobs. He looked from side to side but still couldn't see the source of the noise.

Finally he got down on all fours and peered under Timothy's bed. Curled up at the end of the bed was his little brother. Tim's arms covered his head, as the remainder of his body seemed to be fiercely twitching away.

Rich crawled to where Tim lay crumpled up and slowly carried him out from beneath the bed. They lay there with Rich rocking Tim from side to side as he kept saying "It's all right, Tim, nobody is going to hurt you."

It took almost a half hour before the twitching stopped and the sad voice quieted.

Rich didn't ask anything of his brother, but slowly Timothy began to speak.

"I was on the living room floor watching television and they were in the kitchen shouting at each other and drinking that stuff they liked to drink. I don't know why but he came over and shut off the show I was watching."

Tim stopped talking but Rich knew there had to be more to the story.

"Come on Tim what happened then"

Tim's response was directed away from Rich. He seemed to be ashamed of what had transpired.

"Catherine was at school when he came over to me and began to hit me and hit me until Edith shouted for him to stop hitting me, and when he wouldn't, she got up and left the house. She slammed the front door real loud as she left. He gave me a real hard kick that hurt me so bad. I rolled under the bed. I don't know when he went away, but I have been hiding here forever. "

To make Tim happier, Rich focused his talk on the fact that soon Rich would be taking Timothy back to New York to be with him. Then they would be permanently reunited.

"But, Rich, I can't go away with you. I know there is something very dumb about me. I don't know what it is and, anyway, Poppa will find me, and boy would he give me a licking."

"No, Timmy, that's not true. There is nothing wrong with you. You are the nicest guy I know."

Rich always called his brother Timmy when he was trying to make his younger brother feel good about himself.

"You may be different from some others, but we are all a bit different from one another. I would rather have you at my side than anybody else."

"No, Rich. I love you and I think you love me, but I do such dumb things so often and there are times when I just don't want to say anything. What scares me most is that I'm afraid of almost everything. The only person I really like to be with is you, and when you are away, I even hate myself."

He was crying now and ever so slowly he walked away from his brother.

What Tim had just said was not the first time Rich had heard them. On the one hand, he applauded the brain power Tim showed with those words, but, on the other hand, he cringed at the thought of the torment Tim must go through every day with the realization of what he was. His love for his little brother brought forth a fiercely uttered decision.

"Now listen to me. You are right. I'm as unhappy as you are when I'm away from you. So here's what we are going to do right now. You're going to pack up all your clothes and I'm not going to unpack either of my two cases. Then we're going to fly out of this dreadful house and get our asses up to my place in New York."

"But don't you need money to get to New York?"

"I've got that covered. This past week I was chosen to do two national commercials that will run and run and run. Many dollars will flow into my pockets. So you and I are going to pack up all your stuff, and we are going to catch the five o'clock flight to New York.

Tim jumped high in the air a huge smile on his face. He then began to joyously scream out time after time, "Me and you – Me and you – Me and you. Hooray, Hooray!"

And then the sadness seemed to creep over him again. He turned to Rich and almost pleadingly asked, "Will I have to go to school?"

"You wouldn't want to do something that you dislike would you?"

A very rapid "Not a chance" spilled from Tim's mouth. "Not a chance."

"That's fine with me."

Tim paused for several seconds and then an even greater smile broke open on his face and he shouted out, "Okay. We got a deal."

In less than one hour they had gathered all of Tim's things and left without so much as leaving a note.

Ben and Edith returned home some hours later. It wasn't until late that next morning that they wondered what had happened to Timothy. It was with great relief that they realized he had probably wandered off. They presumed he would return in due time but welcomed his absence. They never reported his being missing.

As a matter of fact they were rather delighted that they had no idea of where or how they could contact either of their sons.

Chapter Six

Tim loved the flight to New York, and upon arrival at the tiny apartment Rich had rented for them, he spent the first three days peering through the window that overlooked Seventh Avenue and Forty Sixth Street looking up and down at the warfare that seemed to be going on below him.

At first he was certain that all the noise and total chaos which went on, be it night or day, was going to drive him crazy and that he would never go down to the street and the madness below him. Sometimes a gentle hum would seep through to him, and he would think of going down to the street below. It was if people down below were humming up to him and he would enjoy their gentle voices.

What amazed him most was that he began to understand some of the gibberish that filtered up to their apartment, and he would be able to decipher the New Yorker's tongue as it reached his ears. From there, enjoyment seemed to emerge, and, every so often, he began to think there was some pleasure he could derive by joining the madness below him.

Even the smells that drifted into their apartment brought different odors depending upon the time of day. He finally decided he liked the night better because it was somewhat quieter at night. It was as if a Peace God ruled in the darkness below.

Each morning Rich would take Tim for a walk through the neighborhood. He once tried to go out by himself but the number of cars, the noises that were always exploding around him, the odd looking people who would often look up to him and then start shouting out words that he could not in any manner understand terrified him as they swiftly brushed by him.

What would be most terrifying were the short, fat women who would spit out volumes of words in some language he could not understand. He combined that with imploring gestures that backed up those words that had no meaning to him. It took him a long time to relax in this world that at times seemed so foreign to him.

On occasion, Rich would take him to Central Park. This brought great joy to Tim. He loved to just stare at the trees and he picked several really huge ones that particularly excited him. He would stare up to these goliaths and shout out to them as he was walking away. "I love you trees."

The trees never responded, but as he walked away he always added another "I love you trees. I hope you like me."

Chapter Seven

The TV commercials kept Rich's bank account filled over with heavy duty checks. However, he also learned that being a tight-assed spendthrift was the smart way to handle one's dollars. His spending for anything frivolous was a rare event. But knowing he had a goodly amount of wealth, allowed him to do something he had long wanted to do.

He made an appointment with the renowned Doctor Charles Cohen who was noted as the leading specialist in the treatment of mentally impaired young people.

The night before going to see, the doctor Rich asked Tim if he would like to tag along the next day when Rich had a doctor's appointment.

"I've never seen a doctor before. Is it fun?"

"I wouldn't call it fun, but it sure is interesting and sometimes they discover something that is good to know about."

Tim pondered the need to see a doctor and then told Rich that he really didn't want to see any doctor.

"Okay, but I'll be leaving at about nine and I won't be back until noon."

As expected, Tim changed his mind the next morning. They left promptly at nine a.m.

Upon entering the doctor's quarters they both were dazzled by what looked more like a handsome apartment than an office space. Beautiful pictures decorated each wall in the room and there were lovely types of plants randomly placed around the entire room.

As they waited for the doctor to join them, Tim was approached by a very pretty nurse who asked him if he would like a Coca Cola. He, of course, was soon sipping away. Moments later, she returned to pick up the now empty glass. She then whispered in his ear that if he agreed to the doctor's doing a simple exam on him, she would soon be bringing him a huge vanilla ice cream cone.

Tim asked if it could be chocolate instead, to which the nurse readily agreed.

After the introductions and a discussion of the weather, the doctor walked in smiling away at the two young boys he was looking forward to meeting. His first real question was directed to Rich.

"Rich, is there anything serious bothering you today?"

With a hidden wink and a sly smile the doctor alerted Rich to the fact that he knew Tim was the real patient who was to be examined.

"I think I am doing rather well, but as I haven't had a physical in quite some time and since Tim tagged along, I thought it would be a good idea if Tim and I were both examined."

"And you, Timothy, how is your health?"

Tim honestly reported that he didn't have a clue as to how he was feeling.

"Well, Timothy, do you often get fatigued during the day?"

"I don't know how to answer that because I am not sure what that word 'fatigued' means."

"Oh, that is just a silly word that a doctor uses to impress his patients. Please excuse me for that. What I want to know is do you get tired a lot?"

Tim nodded his head.

"Well, Tim, can I tell you something? I get tired all the time. I don't like getting that way, but I've gotten used to it. Do you like it when you get tired?"

Tim's response was slow in emerging, but he finally detailed that when he was tired, he would do dumb things. He would get angry at himself and everybody else.

"I don't know for sure, but I am happier when I am not tired. Why is that?"

"Tim, I have the same problem, and I absolutely hate myself for that. The way I stop it is to count from one to ten, and then I laugh at myself for being such a dummy. You might want to try that sometime. It might work. Laughing at myself always makes me feel better."

He then turned to Rich asking him how well they got along with their parents.

"I should have told you that Tim and I left our parents to come to New York. The answer to your question is that they were beastly animals that I have always hated. Tim and I were born to them and that is the last good thing they did for us."

"And, Tim, do you feel the same way as Rich does?"

Tim fidgeted a long time before he answered that his parents were the people who made him feel the worst.

"I think they enjoyed making me cry."

The doctor paused for a minute or two. He then said that on the information sheet that they had filled in, they mentioned an older sister and wondered how they felt about her.

Rich turned to his brother and told him to be the first to answer that question.

"Catherine likes only one thing and that is when she hits me or pinches me, and I start to cry."

To which Rich added, "That's sums her up perfectly."

"Tim, do you like your father and mother?"

"I don't like anybody who still lives in our place back home."

The doctor swiftly switched the remainder of the examination to a long series of questions that primarily stayed with personal matters. The questions were always first directed to Rich and then asked of Tim.

Most of Tim's responses were often far off target or disliked and, therefore, not answered. The simpler the question that Tim received, the more complex Tim's response became. The end of each answer always brought with it a direct look at Rich who would always give Tim a big smile and a thumbs up. Thus reinforced, Tim became more and more at ease with each question.

Eventually, both brothers were given several basic physical tests. Dr. Cohen nodded at Rich who quickly picked up the message that clearly stated this is for Tim.

The good doctor aimed his next question at Tim when he said. "My goodness what are you doing in a doctor office? You are as healthy as can be. I can't understand why you brothers came to see me. Tim, is there anything you can tell me what makes you feel the worst?"

"When Ben or Edith yell at me or hit me. They don't ever say so but Rich told me that they were my Mother and Father."

"Do you like Ben and Edith?"

Tim first looked to Rich who nodded his head.

In a very low voice Tim answered: "Well, I know I'm supposed to like them like I love Rich but I don't. They are always shouting at me and hitting me for something I have done, even if it was the first time I did it. That makes me feel bad and then I cry."

"Could you tell me about those bad things?"

"Rich, can I tell him bad things about myself?"

"Tim, you can tell him anything you want to because, in my opinion, you have never done anything really bad."

"Okay, here goes. Sometimes a mean person will make fun of me. They say it over and over and keep calling me bad names like dummy. I run away from them and when I am far enough from them, I might pee on the sidewalk or start a fire or throw a rock through a window, and then I have to run away as fast as I can so that no one else will hit me."

"Well, Tim, let me teach you something. It was the people who made fun of you that were the bad people. And here is how you can handle those happenings. First off, you really should always be walking with someone you know. I doubt that anyone will talk to you when you are accompanied by a friend."

"But sometimes I like to walk around the street where we live. Rich says it is okay for me do so."

"Well in that case here's what I would do. Turn away from those bad people without saying a word and very slowly stroll away. When you have walked about twenty or thirty feet away, take a brief look back at them. You don't say a word just look at them as if they were the most stupid people in the world. Smile at them, give them one pitying sneer, then turn away as you continue your walk."

"Is it okay if I first ask you a question?"

"Sure. I like your questions."

"What does the word 'sneer' mean?"

"Well if you want to say something bad to someone you don't like, curl up your lips like this and laugh. That's a sneer."

The doctor made such a funny face that Tim started laughing at the doctor and shouted out, "Oh, I like that."

All three joined in laughter at the very funny face now being made by each of them.

The doctor was the first to partially wipe the grin off his face as he asked, "Tim, here's one last question for you. Do you like to watch television?"

"I sure do."

"That's good. You sound great to me and very normal, but there is something that troubles me about Rich that I would like to check out. I think I can get more out of him if I can spend a few minutes alone with him. Would you mind if I asked my assistant to take you to the TV room and see if there is any food out there that you might enjoy?"

Tim's face lit up as he turned to Rich and told him that he really was hungry but he wouldn't be eating too much, so he would still be hungry for lunch no matter what they would be offering him.

Chapter Eight

As the door closed behind Timothy, the doctor frowned and asked Rich how long Tim had been in this state. "Always," was the one word response.

The doctor then asked Rich to tell him in truly honest terms what their parents were like.

"My parents are beyond definition. You're referring to the two most self-centered ignoramuses in the entire world who believe it is a good thing to display fornication at its vilest directly to their children? Need I say more?"

"How did you survive them?"

"I have hated them from as early as I can remember, but my real distaste for them grew when I saw how they treated my delight, my brother, Tim. You know something, Doctor, I really believe there is something beautiful and wonderful hiding in Tim's body. But our parents go out of their way to trample on all his goodness."

"I presume you would like to murder them?"

"There was a time when I dreamt of killing them, but I have just done something far better. I've stolen Tim away from that mad twosome. They will never again manage to harm him in any way."

"Tell me more about Tim."

"To me he has only one problem. It centers on his brain. There are times when he is the sweetest person in the world, and seconds later he can get lost and cry or try to set a fire or any number of other wild things, and then he suddenly changes back to being the sweetest kid in the world."

"Is there any pattern to the things that he does?"

"No. We never know what may come forth from him, and I certainly do not know what causes the eruptions. Though I really believe that when he is at ease with himself, there couldn't be a sweeter kid in the world."

"Has he ever had a breakdown where he would weep or scream or completely shut himself off from anyone in the room with him?"

"Far too many times. The worst he has ever gotten is when he disappears into a world of his own and there is nothing we can do to bring him back to us. Those times are rare but frightening. The scariest thing about that is his abrupt return to us. It's as if he had journeyed off to some crazed place but doesn't know that he has been away."

The doctor took Rich's hands and squeezed them.

"All of that confirms what I had been thinking of. Your brother is afflicted with a dreadful disease but, fortunately for him, it is far from the really destructive form of that disease. He can lead a life with some pleasures awaiting him even if his brain capacity is severely limited."

He then went into a lecture that he very much hated giving.

"The sad news is that I don't believe he will ever get any better. I doubt that your brother will ever live a life close to normalcy."

Richard began to sink further into his chair as he listened.

"His ease with speaking and the vastness of his vocabulary are astonishing. But his funny little shuffle and his explosiveness is startling. Couple those factors with his ever constant mood changes, leads me to believe he is suffering from a relatively new disease, named Asperger's Syndrome. It is a form of Autism and, in all probability, it is almost impossible to cure. I am much troubled by the fatigue factor which I believe is stronger than what he says. Have you noticed it at all?"

"Yes. There are times when he seems to be looking at you and involved with the conversation, and, but seconds later, his eyes close and he is gone. His worst times occur when he is tired."

Dr. Cohen then launched a series of rapid fire questions at Rich.

"Does he wring his hands or twist his fingers? Does he often have trouble in social situations? Does he insist on getting dressed in one way only? Does he avoid eye contact when talking to you? Does he seem overly concerned about the weather? Is he so good at arithmetic and music that he astonishes you at times?"

One word answers were fired back as quickly as they had been sent out. Each answer was a simple "Yes, Sir."

"Let me ask you a very personal question. Do you love Tim?

"I have loved Tim since the very first I saw him and that love has grown every day since."

"Does he know that you love him?"

"That's a strange question, and I sure don't know how to answer it."

"Well then let me tell you why I ask the question. Tim suffers most from insecurity. That lack of self-approval is his biggest enemy. He has no inner sense of worth and the whole world leaves him totally unaware as to who he is and what he is. The only thing he is sure of is that everyone else in the world is different from him. He has no sense of good or bad and, worst of all, it drives him slightly mad. What he needs is someone who can, in every way, show him that he is loved and therefore is a worthwhile being. From what you tell me, I assume you are the only person who loves him. That love must be clearly known and appreciated by Tim. At least he will know that someone cares for him and therefore he must be a pretty good guy."

"I assure you, Doctor. That will be the easiest task I have ever been asked to perform. I adore Tim, and he knows that I love him and will always be there for him."

"I couldn't hear sweeter words but now let's go on with more dire words. I am certain that your brother is a victim of Asperger's, and I don't have any simple answer for him. It is very similar to Autism, but is considered to be slightly less destructive than that horrific disease. I don't buy into that theory. Both diseases are equally horrific. He has a strength that is fortunate. His speaking ability is a hope and a blessing. I would next try to get him into reading, but, unfortunately, there is no medicine that I can prescribe for him."

The doctor paused to let all the information he had fed Rich to sink in for the young man. Rich's head had bowed down as if the doctor had beaten him. Slowly he raised his head as he plaintively asked the doctor if that was all.

"No, Rich, there is much more, and none comes with any promising words. You have a very sick brother but he is fortunate in two ways. One, he seems to like himself and the second is that he likes to laugh. They are more important to him than any medicine I might prescribe for him."

"I think I've always known that but I wonder if there is anything else I can do for him."

"Yes. Keep on talking to him and keep letting him know that you love him, and let him realize that love matters – and, believe me, it really does. He senses that you love him and that gives him a belief in himself. Don't treat him as if he was just another rather ill child but always know that he is a sick young boy. Get him interested in reading simple books with plots that are easily understood. Be prepared to fail in that effort, while praising him for being such a good reader. It could open a new world to him, but don't be disappointed if he finds nothing appealing in reading."

The doctor took another pause to allow Rich to absorb what he had just heard.

He resumed with what he considered to be the most action that Rich must provide for Tim.

"Treat him always as a person of value. Never stop loving him, and make certain that he knows that you will always be there for him. He will always need and prosper with the care you provide. He, in turn, will forever reward you with endless love and devotion. The joy you supply him with will prove that you love him, and he needs that love to sustain himself. Show him constant displays of joy and pleasure at being in his company. Never forget that he has a dreadful disease that will never leave him."

Rich felt as if he were just stabbed in the heart.

The doctor was relentless in burdening Rich with what he must know about his brother. The direst moments came when he started telling Rich of the dreadful ailments that could attack Tim.

"I am certain that if I ask you when he is at his best you will say 'when he is happy.' On the other hand if I were to ask you when is he at his worst, I am certain you will say when he is depressed, and you will be spot on. Does he often seem to fall into a deep depression?"

"Very rarely, but when he does, it is a fearful time for all of us."

"Well, that is the best news I could have heard. Though he does seem to suffer from Asperger's be grateful that it seems to be a very mild form of same. You must learn to be ever on the alert for what he is going through. When he is stricken with even the slightest form of depression, it can be brutally effective in bringing him down."

The good doctor paused there as he watched Rich take in these dire words.

He paused for a brief moment before starting with more troubling words.

"There is only one way for you to help him, and that is by constantly reassuring him of his value as a great human being. Keep telling him of your deep love for him. He has no sense of worth and accordingly is filled with anger about who and what he is. He loves you and is envious of what and who you are. You must always be aware of the moments when he may drift into feelings of self –depression. Depression can be brutally destructive for him and anyone who loves him."

"I strongly believe that Tim has never fallen off from being a wonderful kid."

"Listen to me. It may never happen or it might happen tonight and, if so, then you must attack him with every weapon available to you. Should such a horror attack Tim, you must immediately jump on him with every sweetness and diversionary tactics available to you. Every time one of those moods attack him, they will become more frequent and more dangerous. It won't be easy to divert him but if you have to do wild body flips, or any other manic items, do it and save his life. There is no easy way out of that battle."

The doctor raised his head and took Rich's hands.

"Let me repeat myself. There is one tactic on your part that I believe you have already chosen to use. Make certain he knows that every moment of everyday he knows that you love him, and that you will always love him. It will give him a strength to rely on that no pill could offer up. Believe me when I tell you that I hate myself when I confess that I just do not have any other answer than what I have said, about love and praise for what a great guy he is, being the only offering that can help him."

Rich's face filled with tears.

"Fear is his greatest enemy. I don't have a clue as to what causes fear to capture Tim but I am certain that when it does assail him he is a lost young man. You have come to me for answers, and the truth of the matter is that my offerings are pitiful. Other than always talking softly to him and with a gay laugh in your voice, there is nothing I can prescribe which can ease his woes. Do know that it is mandatory in everything you say to him that they only convey happy thoughts and belief in him. Getting him to laugh at you is likely to produce wonders in him."

They both sat there knowing there was nothing more that could be said.

It took quiescent moments before Rich ventured, "He is basically a good soul. Is that the best we can expect of him?"

"In all probability, the answer is yes. Did he ever go to school?"

"Barely one month."

"Did his fellow students often abuse him?"

"They did so every moment of every day."

"Tell me something, Richard. I know I haven't offered up much for you, but why have you waited so long to get help for your brother?"

"I never had the money, and our parents controlled Tim. This is the first chance that I have been able to do what I think is right for him."

"I can see that he does speak quite adequately. Am I right?"

"Oh yes. If he likes the person he is talking to he can gab away. Then again, if he is frightened by a person, he won't so much as say one word to that person. He never speaks to our sister, our parents, or anyone he thinks may hurt him. Most people he just ignores."

"That's par for the course. The happier he is, the more hope there is that he might have an almost pleasant life. But that life could be short and definitely will be filled with times of great despair. That is a common symptom that identifies him as an Asperger's sufferer."

Tears started welling up in Rich's eyes, but the good doctor waved them away.

"Don't give up on the boy. He has two things going for him. He shows amazing signs of intellect. You are obviously bright. I believe he too possesses the capability to think wisely. It is a different manner of thinking, but it may be one that could serve him well. And he has you. It is obvious that he loves you and is totally at ease with you. That is a strong tool and a great obligation for you. Don't ever forget that obligation."

For the first time that morning, Rich felt a spark of hope. He more than adored his little brother and totally believed that he was sent here to be Tim's hope.

"Well, Doctor, we may not have accomplished much, but I've seen great promise with Tim and you."

The doctor quickly cut him short.

"No. Tim is a much troubled lad, and I doubt that I can be of any real help for him. Most of the time his illness will keep him far from where we would want him to be. You can help him most by never berating him for doing something that is otherwise normal for him. Kid him, tease him, laugh with him but never get into a serious subject with him. Just keep him laughing at the world. Don't waste your time and money with me or any other so-called specialist. You are Timothy's only hope. Don't delude yourself about the potential of things turning around and getting better. They won't. Just pray that it never gets any worse."

The doctor ended the meeting with further advice on giving Tim as much freedom as is sensible.

"May I advise you to keep Tim away from children who are a little younger or a bit older than him. They can be vicious in their attacks on those they feel are vulnerable. When he feels confident about himself, he will enjoy his life. You must leave him to be what he is and, in the doing, save yourself."

That afternoon the boys treated themselves to a spaghetti dinner. In the middle of devouring the meal, Tim turned to Rich and exclaimed that he liked that doctor and wondered how soon they would be going to see the doctor again.

Rich very casually replied that since the doctor said there wasn't anything wrong with either of them, why spend money for a doctor they did not need and that going to a baseball game was more fun and far cheaper than the doctor.

Tim heartedly agreed.

Chapter Nine

Shortly after their doctor's meeting, Rich received a phone call which singularly altered his life. It came from the producer who had advised him to get up to New York.

He told Rich that he had just heard that the producers of the hit musical 'La Cages aux Folles' was about to refill the role of the young son in the play,

"It's a great part and I know that you were born to make it yours. Be at my office tomorrow at nine-thirty and I'll give you all the info on how to get that part. Don't disappoint me."

Within two hours after said meeting, Rich had his first Broadway audition. Within the next week Rich Morton had captured a legitimate role in a show that was a guaranteed smash hit. To his delight, the prestigious New York Times notice on his performance was as close to a rave as the Times ever got.

Tim had cut the review from the paper and would stop one and all as he showed the tribute about his brother.

Anyone passing him on the street, be they friends or strangers, had to pause to read the piece as Tim would advise them, "He's my brother."

There wasn't a happier man in New York City than Richard Morton. The review got him a raise in salary and esteem from all in the cast. Everything he had ever dreamed of was coming his way, and what particularly delighted him was that his brother, Tim, seemed to share the joy. It mattered not that Timothy never understood what the review meant. What did matter is that Timothy seemed to sense the joy everybody was sharing and, therefore, he should be happy too.

After much discussion between Rich and Timothy, they decided to send a copy of the Times review to their parents. Included with that review was a one hundred dollar bill and a note that indicated that amount would be forthcoming each month so long as they never were to be, in any form, contacted by either parent.

They did not include their new address in said letter. That letter was never answered.

Rich's laughter was the heartiest.

"I guess one of them got the note and didn't tell the other one about the money. We'll never again hear from either of them."

Chapter Ten

One afternoon Rich walked off the stage, smiling about how well the Wednesday matinee had gone. Phil, the stage manager of 'La Cage,' flagged him down and told Rich that there was a woman backstage who wanted to see him.

"Mind your P's and Q's because she is a Casting Director for the Oregon Shakespeare Festival."

Rich had heard of that theatre, but had not a clue as to why this woman was asking to see him. He was more than slightly ill at ease about the forthcoming meeting with this important stranger.

The stage manager took Rich to a very handsome woman waiting patiently in the wings. "Rich, this is Molly Fields. She knows more about theatre than you ever will, so don't try to B.S. her."

And with that he left the two alone.

"It's my pleasure to meet you, Richard. I saw today's matinee, and I must commend you for a very fine performance."

"Thanks for the kind words but the author wrote a perfect part, and even I could not foul it up."

"Yes, the part was lovely, but you made it sing and you deserve the accolades you are receiving. But let's stop talking about you. Has Phil told you that I work for the Oregon Shakespeare Festival? Do you know much about us?"

Rich acknowledged that he had heard good things about the company but not much in detail.

"Well, hold on as I rave about the Shakespeare Festival and what we do. What we stage year in and year out is pure perfection. I love that we grew from the smallest of theatrical groups to where we are today as one of the outstanding theatre purveyors in the entire country. Please excuse me if I bore you about what we have accomplished. You can shut me up by just saying 'enough already.'"

Her love for the Festival was evident when she launched into the history of her company.

"We played initially in a tiny outdoor theatre that played before maybe a few hundred people who sat on wooden benches. It all started in 1893 when our first Chautauqua was staged."

Rich interrupted Molly by raising his hand and sheepishly asking, "Pardon my stupidity, but I don't have a clue as to what that word 'Chautauqua' means."

"Oh, for goodness sake, I am a ninny. Nobody today knows what a Chautauqua is, and as a matter of fact I didn't have a clue about what it meant until I got my job with the Festival. Simply stated it is a form of entertainment that started across our country sometime late in the 19th Century. Its purpose was to bring entertainment to smaller communities throughout the states. Sometimes it was with theatrical performances, but it could also be just speakers or musicians or preachers or musicians or any number of other events that could attract an audience. In Ashland it simply meant the performance staged would always be that of a Shakespeare play."

Rich politely listened and was not knocked out by what he heard.

"Summer after summer nothing changed. The featured event was always a Shakespeare show. This lasted until a very young man named Angus Bowmer was hired by the small local college to join their faculty as a teacher of stage arts. He also directed the three annual stage productions at the school. Everyone in town was singularly impressed with how much better the productions became."

She went on in some detail to describe how Bowmer had radicalized every event staged at the college. This in turn, meant directing the summer Chautauqua production which meant a new way of staging the annual production of a Shakespeare play. By 1905 the summer theatre had been enlarged to accommodate fifteen hundred devoted fans. By 1917 a more modern theatre delighted its ever growing audience and renowned people such as John Phillips Sousa and William Jennings Bryan appeared on the stage.

Richard was properly impressed with what had happened so many years ago but couldn't understand what this was going to lead to.

"And is this what is still done in Ashland?"

"Thank you, Richard, I do tend to be a bit long winded. Let's get to today. We start performances in late February and close in late October. Add rehearsal time and, from the actors point of view, that means almost a solid year of being paid for doing something you would probably do for nothing. Each of our actors have the chops to star in any production from New York to Los Angeles. For us it means we stress perfect casting and a totally congenial acting company."

She segued into how consistently great each of their productions were and how hard they strive to be as close to perfection with each of the eleven shows they stage each year.

"I'll allow that occasionally we might not reach the heights we always strive for, but we are never far off."

Miss Fields then launched into a history of what had happened to the theatre since Angus Bowmer came to this delightful little city.

She talked with fervor of the two love affairs that occurred as Bowmer fell in love with the potential of a legitimate theatre thriving in Ashland, while Ashland fell in love with this enthusiastic work he presented each year in their town.

For many years, Bowmer always opened the summer season on July Fourth for two weeks. Each production was singularly noticed by the townspeople, by the increase of tourism, and money flowing into town because of the great success of 'Theatre in Ashland.'

But Bowmer had much more in mind for himself and Ashland. It took many years to become a reality, but all of Ashland agreed with him and encouraged his pushing for a great Ashland theatre. On July 2, 1935, the Oregon Shakespeare Festival officially opened with a production of 'Twelfth Night' in the new theatre that seated over six hundred attendees.

They offered a golden package to lovers of the

theatrical world. Each year thereafter the audience grew and grew and grew.

Molly then added "As I've already told you today, we stage eleven shows of varied genre and, yes, the prices are sky high which enable us to bring in actors of talents as good as anyone on Broadway. The bottom line of it all is that we celebrate the success of Bowmer's dream."

She continued detailing the path that had been taken and how their dreams and fame spread throughout the West coast. Today visitors from all over the world see magnificent shows performed in the most modern of theatres. At least four Shakespeare productions are presented each year amidst a total of eleven diverse plays."

Rich jumped in by saying that the Festival was known today by every actor he knew. "Hey, you people are a legend. Every actor I know would love to work there."

Word of the theatrical wonders that were being presented in Ashland became legendary throughout the country. An Eastern drama critic once wrote that the best Shakespearean productions in the United States were to be seen In Ashland, Oregon.

Two important groups fought to get to the Festival. Far better actors were desperate to get roles there and theatre goers in ever increasing numbers flocked to productions staged by the Festival.

It brought a huge economic boom upon this sweet little city.

Molly concluded pitching the values of where she worked in a most gentle tone. "Today's Oregon Shakespeare Festival is a roaring success with even bigger dreams for the future. Working there is a pure delight and that is what I want to talk about with you."

Rich turned slightly pale as he heard those words.

"Please, just one second there! I have a great part in a great play all the while working on Broadway and making more money than I ever dreamt I could be making. And you are asking me to leave all of that?"

"Of course not, I am here to acquaint you with who we are and to learn what your talents are, and whether or not in the near future we might fall in love with one another.

She was the first to laugh and soon they were at ease laughing at one another as they continued their joyful tussle about whether Rich should so much as consider the Ashland Theatre as worthy of his talents and, of course, vice versa.

Molly then described her job as a year-in-year-out pursuit of actors capable of delivering performances that would stun their fellow actors and a very knowledgeable audience. She then added, "Of course you know that we are not just a Shakespeare house – we produce all sorts of dramatic pieces.

"I come to you because of 'The Times' review and what others have said about you. After seeing your work today, I know you are one talented soul."

She then described the committee of eight she headed that had almost total approval rights as to who got approval to perform on Ashland's Oregon Shakespeare Festival stage.

"We are a very demanding bunch, and you must obtain unanimous approval from all on this group. Our standards are very high, and that's why I would like you to visit our little town and meet the remainder of our group. We will pay you the cost of getting there and back. I needn't tell you in advance that we are a tough bunch to impress, but you will be given our decision rapidly. Seeing your performance today told me a great deal. I feel confident in your chances with our team of creative snobs."

She then went into detail about how hard they all worked to assure perfect casting for every role in every play.

"If I do meet your standards, and I am invited to perform with your company, what are the pay standards?"

She spelled out what one normally was paid at Rich's level but went on to add that the figure one is paid varies from actor to actor.

"Obviously, Broadway pays a good deal more than what we can afford, but Ashland is far cheaper to live in. Yes, our actors are judged by their talents but their human traits are equally important. There are no prima donnas tolerated in our company."

"However, I guarantee that if you are invited to perform at Ashland you, like most of our company, will be fighting tooth and nail to maintain your position with the Festival."

Richard was torn apart. He knew that this could be a huge break for him, but he also knew that his responsibilities to Tim had to be observed whether it be in New York or Ashland.

"Look, I have a brother who is quite ill. He has an ailment that requires constant care. He needs me in his life. And, truthfully, I need him in my life. The first time he looked up at me, he smiled, and I knew I adored him. I am happy when my brother is happy. It is the only thing in my life that really matters. You know Ashland. I don't. If he can't fit into Ashland, then I must turn you down."

"Wait one second right there. I have been woefully neglect by not telling you the most important part of your coming to Ashland."

"And what would that be."

"Well, sit back. I have a magical tale to tell you. It may take some time in the telling, but when I am done, you will accuse me of lying about our wonderful city. Every word will be true and most important is that there is no city in the whole wide world that could be better for your brother. Give him one month in Ashland, and he will know all the streets and depend on most of the people who populate our town."

She opened her purse and pulled out a large folded sheet. She unfolded the sheet revealing a beautiful scene of a night shot of a theatre performing a play open to the sky.

"Now this is a shot of a theatre hard at work one night. So I ask you a question. Where is this theatre located?"

Rich studied the photo looking at every side of it.

"Well I assume it is one of your theatres in Ashland and, with the look of things, I would say it is on the outskirts of town just before the local forest embraces it."

"Yes, you are right on about it being a theatre in Ashland, but you are dead wrong about its location. This is our Elizabethan Theatre which is located in the heart of our beautiful city and that is what Ashland looks like which is one tree filled street after another. The population is about twenty two thousand and every citizen and non-citizen loves our Ashland. It is a beautiful little city that is surrounded by majestic mountains and beautiful forests. Wherever you live in town or outside of it, you can lose yourself in the beauties of wondrous trees, magnificent flowers and the residents that love the city they live in."

She finished by saying, "I would look forward to meeting your brother, and I know he would thrive in Ashland."

"I was hoping I could talk you into doing so. My place is but a few blocks from here and, if I say so myself, I am a great cook. May we throw together a little meal for you?"

"I'm in town with one of my fellow committee members. If you can handle him also I think it would be fun."

"There's no difference between cooking for three or cooking for four so we would love to have him join us."

"Great! I am sick and tired of eating in another over-priced restaurant. A home cooked meal sounds perfect to me."

"Then it's a deal. Just come in with a smile on your face and speak softly. Timothy is really not totally at ease with new folk, but if you enter his life as a friend of the family, he will instantly adopt you as one of his best friends."

"Then do give me your address, and I'll see you in an hour."

Chapter Eleven

The evening proved to be a roaring success. Rich had prepared Tim with the news that they were having guests for dinner who were very nice people.

"I don't know them too well, but what I do know says they are our kind of people."

Molly and her associate, Scott Wilson, arrived promptly at 5:00 p.m. carrying a bottle of good wine and an even larger bottle of Dr. Pepper. Both brothers could not have been more pleased with the gifts.

Timothy's first utterance was directed at the guests as he asked if they always spoke so softly.

Scott replied that loud voices bothered him but he could speak louder if that is what Tim preferred.

"No, no. This is just the way I like to talk but most people seem to be screaming at me, and I don't like that."

"Well then, Tim, we will speak as if we were birds gathering for a quiet discussion about whether or not it was a good day for flying.

Tim didn't know that expression and wondered whether or not he liked those words but a smile slowly grew on his face and he decided he liked what he had heard.

"Scott, I like you."

There was nothing that could prevent this evening from being a huge success.

Molly embarked on a simple history of the old Ashland which included the fact that this tiny town's original name was Ashland Mills. It was so named to honor the fact that the bulk of the residents hailed from Ashland, Kentucky. Also, early on two equally important events occurred. The first was a Water Mill that was completed almost simultaneously with the construction of the equally important Flour Mill. Both Mills were most successful in making life infinitely easier for the pioneers living there.

The Water Mill provided safe water and the other was the opening of an equally important flour mill which was great help in providing solid food for all in town and also became a vital economic factor.

Its first residents, numbering about fifty men, women and children, were all proud of this new city called Ashland Mills.

It remained thus for many years until new residents felt those doings no longer reflected anything of great importance, so the word 'Mills' was dropped. The time had come to modernize the city and it was renamed Ashland, Oregon.

With this iteration, joy obviously dominated all.

The evening's meal cut short the conversation, as all turned to the meal that Rich had cooked. The food occupied the conversation and all were less than pleased when they realized it was past seven and the party was subjected to an abrupt end.

As they left, Molly asked if they and Rich could meet sometime the next morning.

"I think I have the answer to a question that was untouched this afternoon. The question you left unasked, and should you not have recalled it, was about whether you and Tim would enjoy living in our little town. So what say we meet at eleven at the restaurant that's just around the corner?"

"That is fine with me. I'll first take my morning walk with Tim and then be yours."

On that note the little party ended. The guests left and Rich took off for the theatre where his play was killing the audiences.

Tim suggested that he could do the cleaning from this evening's party now, but Rich laughingly told his brother that he was not earning sufficient money to replace the plates and glasses that would surely be broken in that effort.

Tim finished off his Dr. Pepper, turned on the TV, and instantly fell asleep in the chair facing the commercial laden set.

Some four hours later Rich's return home set off another ritual chore he did each evening as he awakened Tim and then proceeded to tell him about that night's performance and that his part had gone very well.

As they were putting on their PJ's, Tim turned to his brother and told him that he sure liked Molly and Scott

They both fell asleep with smiles on their faces. Tim smiled with the memory of what a happy night this had been, while Rich kept thinking how much of the party Tim had been involved with, and that here it was some four hours later, and Tim still remembered both names of the new people who had entered his life.

The next morning Molly opened their meeting with a short statement imparted to Rich. It consisted of one sentence.

"Your brother will adore Ashland. "

"Why are you so confident in saying that?"

"Simple enough. Last night he went on at some length about his love of the outdoors and how he could tell which tree is which tree by just hugging the tree and smelling it. He went on and on about those smells. Throughout his talking about trees he never stopped smiling."

She then went on to tell Rich that the nickname of Ashland was 'The City of Trees.' She continued to challenge him as she told him that when he visited Ashland he should first take a peek at the glorious mountains that surround Ashland.

"You won't be able to see one barren spot on our streets. Or may I offer an even bolder test. There are some four supermarkets in our town, each of them with varying sized parking lots which share the space between their shoppers' cars and magnificent trees which add beauty and shade to said lots."

The smile that graced his face when he heard those words was as big a smile as he had ever worn.

He wanted to keep asking further questions, but he knew there was nothing more to ask. This Ashland could well be the perfect city for Tim, while being the perfect theatrical experience for himself.

He rushed back to Tim right after his meeting with Molly. He spoke glowingly of this little city called Ashland.

"It is just a tiny town that has street after street covered with beautiful trees of all types and that every one of the mountains that surrounds the city is overwhelmed by thousands and thousands of glorious trees."

He expected some glowing reaction on the plentitude of trees that covered Ashland but was shocked when Tim interrupted his talk on the famed green foliage of Ashland by his asking, "Do you know what the population of Ashland is?"

"Why do you ask that?"

"Well it sounds so nice I will want to meet all the people who live there and find out which trees they like the most."

"Funny you should ask that because I asked Molly that very question this morning. She told me it must be some-where between Twenty three and twenty four thousand."

Tim just nodded, accepted the figures and walked off.

That certainly puzzled Rich. He kept thinking that in New York City there were more people and more cars on the street where they lived than in all of Ashland, yet Tim never asked to meet any New Yorkers. It dawned on Rich that his little brother had more brain sense than any of his more loquacious friends.

Tim who had never wanted to meet anyone now wanted to converse with an entire city. He was smiling when he offered his last question, and the smile stayed on his face.

The look on Tim's face astonished his older brother. Rich realized Tim knew that the difference in people is how they treat and enjoy the beauty of nature. Of great impor-tance is being aware of how the people of each city treat and welcome that city.

Chapter Twelve

Two months later, Rich and Tim boarded a plane at New York's LaGuardia Airport and headed off to Medford, Oregon. Ashland was too small a city to warrant having a full-sized airport. Besides that, Medford was but a twenty minute drive from Ashland, and it had a fine airport which had that year been totally redesigned.

It was a six hour trip that first took them from LaGuardia to Chicago and then to Medford. Tim never spoke a single word on the entire trip. He was in total awe of everything from getting on the plane, to staring at the stewardesses, to eating the sparse meals served to him. He stared awestruck at the world beneath them. But, above all, he was captivated when one of the stewardesses, sensing that this was his first air trip, took him to the pilots' area.

His first words spoken as he was reseated were as big and braggadocio as he had ever spoken. "You know, Rich, I think I could learn to fly this plane."

The glass of water that Rich was about to drink flew instead over his face, chest and trousers.

As they disembarked at the Medford Airport, they were pleased to see Scott waving a welcome home sign at them. Heavy hugs and kisses led to a dash to Scott's car, and within moments, it seemed like they were pulling up at their short-term Ashland home.

"It is far from luxurious but is owned by the Festival, and I'm sure if we keep it clean, and the kitchen is always stocked with edibles, you will enjoy it, if only for the weeks we will be here."

Scott also left a schedule of activities for Rich to follow. This included formal meetings with Molly's committee and tickets for six of the eleven shows now being performed.

Tim was also given tickets to the same productions that Rich did, but they both decided to pass on using Tim's tickets when he fell asleep during the early moments of the first show he attended. Rich was astounded at the quality of all he had seen. To him they were right on a par with the Broadway shows he knew of.

Molly told him that was a common reaction because he had not expected to see the level of excellence they turned out each night.

"We are wonderful, but we certainly aren't Broadway."

The learning period they were put through in the weeks they stayed in Ashland was akin to going for a PHD and they both loved every second of it. Tim particularly loved passing strangers on the street who would greet him with a smile on their faces. He was far more accustomed to the New York frowns.

He would walk into a store that was quaintly decorated, and the shop owner offered him a bite of the cookies that were featured on the counter they reposed on. The closest anyone came to trying to sell him something was the short lady salesperson who advised him to stay away from the grey socks for they tended to tear too easily.

After one early morning stroll of the inner city, neither Rich nor Tim felt any qualms about Tim's wandering by himself through the town and wonderful Lithia Park which adjoined the theatre area.

One stroll with Rich through the park and Tim was hooked. Scott told them that the park was designed by John McLaren who had previously designed the wondrous San Francisco Park. It had everything that Tim liked in its 93 acres.

The lake at the top end of the park seemed to be always filled with swimmers of all ages. The Rose Garden and the Japanese Garden competed in beauty. The tennis courts played under huge trees was the most delightful place to fiercely have a go at that sport. The duck pond, the innumerable paths which led up and down, the thousands of flowers that sprinkled themselves throughout the park put a twinkle through the hearts of all.

Tim, on one such walk, found an additional delight just off the beginning of the park. There he found a large number of teen-aged kids who were very strangely dressed but seemed to be having a grand time playing away on guitars and singing out as loudly as they could. He was screaming with delight after each song when one of the girls shouted out to him that he should come at night when the music was really hot.

Each night thereafter, while Rich was seeing yet another show, Tim would spend hours sitting there with his new friends loving every moment of watching and listening to these so friendly entertainers.

By the third day, he discovered it was customary to drop coins into the hats of these artists. He told Rich all about this tradition and Rich filled Tim's pockets with coins. It was the entertainers themselves who advised Tim that spilling all your money into the hat of just one performer was not the best thing to do.

What pleased Rich most was the ease with which everyone greeted him and accepted Tim. Not once did Tim come home without exclaiming about everyone in Ashland being so friendly.

"Everyone in Ashland treats me like I was their brother, and that's sure nice."

Molly had instantly realized how important Tim was to his brother, and therefore she went out of her way in being nice to the younger brother.

"I've had the pleasure of meeting with your brother twice now. He is a delight, though I was puzzled when sometimes he just stopped talking and drifted off. Was it me or is it part of his problem?"

"Actually, that is a problem that he battles with, but he is much improved. Fact of the matter, he has been quite good all the time he has been here. I am pleased that he reacted so well to you. That tells me that he knows you are important here, and he was uncertain how to handle you."

"Well good for him. I like Tim, and I think there isn't a town in the world that is a better fit for him. Let me tell you about another wunderkind that lives here. I don't know if you have ever seen that blind young man who saunters through our town with his cane swirling wildly in front of him?

Rich had to say he had not seen the boy.

"Well you will and when that happens look at how comfortable he seems to be. Nobody bothers him, but everybody he passes is there for him. They care for him as they allow him to do all he wants to do. That young man is quietly watched after by all of Ashland. Tim will get the same treatment, not to intrude on him, but because they all will care for him. Ashland is the perfect town for the two of you."

The Morton boys left Ashland just one week after their arrival. In Rich's pocket was an unsigned contract that assured his appearance in three totally different plays that coming year. Not one role was merely a walk-on, and the total salary earned from those roles was not too far behind what he earned in 'La Cage.'

The temptation to bring his brother to the city with small town wonders and great theatre was a great lure.

The comparison between the two cities was a constant battle for Rich who spent most of his free time weighing his hectic life in New York to the far more peaceful world of Ashland. New York offered great potential for future success whereas expectations for growth from Ashland was miniscule.

It suddenly dawned on Rich that he was always first thinking of his own future when he should concentrate instead on what would make the best life for Tim.

The next day he queried his troubled brother about where he would prefer to live. "Tim, if you could live in New York or Ashland which would you go for?" Tim pondered a while before answering this difficult question.

"That's a tough question, but I think I would say either place would be just fine. As long as I can be with you, it wouldn't matter." That typical bit of pure genius left Rich deep in thought and then it dawned on him. He felt the same way as Tim.

The answer was simple enough. He knew all about New York but little about Ashland. So why not give Ashland a year. If it works for Tim then we will stay there; if not, New York will always open up its crazy arms for us. Tim would be happy anywhere, and I could discover if Ashland theatre was as appealing as the New York stage.

The next day he called Molly and told her he would be mailing her a signed contract that committed him to Ashland for the following year.

She replied, "You should know that we are delighted to take both you brothers for the coming season."

Chapter Thirteen

$\mathcal{E}$arly that fall the Morton boys became residents of Ashland, Oregon.

Several questions bothered them. Where was the best place for them to live? Should it be right in town next to the theatres, or should they live close to the trees that Tim loved so much? They opted for a beautifully treed area that was a twenty minute walk away from the theatre.

Boredom was dangerous for Tim. Being alone brought on fears which could ignite dangerous activities on his part, ergo everything must be done to avoid those fears. They had to find the way to keep him busy and happy.

Strangely enough it was Tim who had no qualms about being alone. Rich, on the other hand, was ever fearful for his brother. He bought Tim a large television, a small recorder player and a dozen very cool CD's. He taught Timothy how to work both pieces of entertainment but it took several weeks for Tim to get them working correctly. He finally learned how to accomplish this huge task and he could sit for hours enraptured by the entertainment that poured forth.

To further ease his mind, Rich got permission that allowed Tim to sit in on every rehearsal. Tim would quietly take a seat in the furthest back row of the theatre. It wasn't too long before he could repeat each line that came flowing from the stage to his attentive ears. When Rich and Tim returned home for further rehearsal of Rich's lines he would handle all the parts but Rich's. At first it seemed like a fun thing to do and that was how it remained for Tim, but soon Rich delightedly realized that, because of Tim, he was learning his lines faster than ever before. Tim's pleasure was his leaning out the window as he watched the world spin by. He kept telling Rich how happy he was.

"Just keep working with me and real soon I'll be ready to walk all over this place and have a great time doing that. This place is nice."

The transition from New York had been as easy as giving up eating hot peppers and instead devouring only chocolate pudding.

Each of the first days in their new home, Tim and Rich would go on exploratory walks through Ashland. They went to the closest grocery and timed how long it took to get there. Equally important, they noted every store they had to pass on the way home.

Rich constantly drilled Tim with the fact that he must remember that they would never be far apart from each other.

"If you ever get nervous about my being away too long you must wait at home and I will soon be there. Always remember that I'll never be away longer than a few hours at a time. I'll have to do a lot of rehearsing my parts for the plays I am in and that may keep me apart from you for a few hours. Just remember I'll always come straight home when I am done."

Rich would have Timothy repeat what he had said at least twice so as to be certain he got the message.

But it was the walks that totally absorbed them. Walking and knowing where one was became Tim's primary occupation. Rich carefully took many, many journeys with Timothy all the while describing in detail every little stop that was different from what they had just passed.

"This first store is where we bring our dirty clothes. It is next door to our building and our apartment is on the first floor up, and there is only one apartment on each floor."

Each day they would go a bit further as the two brothers slowly increased the distance they trod. Each store Tim remembered meant another victory for him.

On the way back, Tim had to repeat what he had learned on the way out. The errors became fewer and fewer.

Getting the neighbors to know and like Tim was an important task. Fortunately, there was an elderly woman living in each of the flats above them. They couldn't be sweeter and soon were competing for the attention of the absolutely wonderful boys who lived beneath them. Apple pies and chocolate cookies kept pouring down from above.

Yes, Tim was still the same troubled young man. He still required much attention. But, at times, he was almost just another very nice independent teenager.

No, he had no need to have a girlfriend nor, for that matter, he did not need a buddy to pal around with. The only person he needed was Rich.

One might say they were equally dependent. Rich needed Tim almost as much as his brother needed him. They were both going through a learning process about this city and the theatres within it. Most importantly, they were learning more and more about themselves.

Within one month they were both at ease with being just two brothers who now were living in Ashland, Oregon.

Chapter Fourteen

*I*t was close to four p.m., and sixteen year old Timothy Morton was standing alone but as tall as he could while facing downward towards a lovely gravestone and gossiping away directly to the stone. It seemed as if he was talking to the gravestone. If one could eavesdrop on the conversation it seemed that he was telling the stone that he and his brother, the great actor, had a job at the festival.

At times his words were quite loud while at other times he whispered away, as if his words were only meant for hearing by the occupant of the grave.

Not ten feet away from Tim, Tony, the supervisor of the Mountain Cemetery, continued to notice this kid with the strange gait who had been wandering around and around the hundreds of gravestones before stopping at this one stone.

He did no harm. He had merely circled throughout the fields gaping at the huge trees and the wonderful treasure of flowers that graced many of the rocks that were scattered around the fields.

He had stopped his pacing at one of Tony's favorite gravesites. His head was bent low as indeed he seemed to be talking to this one stone. Printed rather boldly on the stone was the name 'Michael Rountree.'

What Tony could not know was that Tim had often spent much time talking to the occupant of this particular grave. The size and shape of the stone and the beautiful trees that surrounded it had drawn Tim back to it each day. He felt so at ease with this stone that talking with it seemed very logical. In fact, just yesterday he had told Michael Rountree of how much he loved his older brother Rich.

"He's always nice to me. He never yells at me. I love Rich more than anything in the whole, whole world."

He would then nod his head as if the person he had told of his love for Rich had answered him.

Tony was an Ashland born hard worker who took more than mere pride in how beautiful his cemetery looked. Not many people gave a hoot about the beauty of these grounds. They just stormed in, spent a few moments at one grave site or another and then rushed off. In all his years tending the Mountain Cemetery not a soul had offered a complement to him on the loving care he brought to these grounds.

"Hey, young fella, I'm Tony, the supervisor of this cemetery and I notice you spend a lot of time here. How come."

"How come what?"

The response threw Tony. Is this kid some smart Alec or is he just not too bright. But the boy kept smiling at Tony and the spoken tone showed only kindness. Tony decided the kid must be OK.

"What I mean is are you related to the man who is buried here?"

That question seriously puzzled Tim. He didn't have a clue as how to answer that question. The word 'buried' completely threw him.

His answer ignored the question.

"My brother and I live across the street and I think it is very beautiful here. I try to spend as much time as I can right here. Is it okay if I do that?"

The question was posed so meekly that Tony was taken aback by the boy who was obviously one sweet kid.

"Do you know anything about this place?"

A fearful shaking of the head spurred Tony on.

"Look, I'm pretty busy today but I've got an idea. Why don't I take you to your house and then you come back here early tomorrow morning. I'm usually loose then so I'll be able to tell you a bunch of very interesting stories about the good souls who live here."

"Can I bring my brother with me?"

"You got it."

"What do you mean when you say that?"

This completely threw Tony. He was confused by this lad who seemed genuinely interested in Tony's workplace. Accordingly, he offered no reply but merely repeated the time and place he would be at this spot the next morning.

His words put a large smile on Tim's face and that sealed the deal for him. Tim again repeated "Can I bring my brother with me?"

"Of course. We'll meet then and talk about this cemetery of ours."

Tim was totally excited by this nice man and what he had to say. He could hardly wait for Rich to get home so that he could tell him about his new friend and the beautiful place he worked in.

Chapter Fifteen

Antonio D'Angelo had been born in Ashland. His parents, Giovanni D'Angelo and Maria D'Angelo, who were first cousins, had been born in Florence, Italy. Tony's father was the last of five boys born to the D'Angelo's.

When Giovanni and Maria were just five and three the entire D'Angelo clan, some four families, moved to New York's little Italy.

Giovanni had only one passion. He recalled being about seven years old when he saw a New York cop fly through the air to scoop up a little boy who was about to enter a heavily trafficked New York avenue. A speeding car missed hitting the boy and the policeman by inches.

The boy ended up in the air hoisted there by the arms of the cop who lay on the ground with blood pouring from his head. As soon as the cop lowered the boy to the ground his mother picked up her son and alternating screaming at him while in the softest of tones blessing the policeman in Italian as the wonderful 'politzeano.'

After a few minutes, a police ambulance arrived and the cop was carefully placed into it. Giovanni even thought about going with him.

Thereafter, there was never any doubt but that Giovanni D'Angelo would someday become an officer of the law.

Giovanni and Maria married when both turned twenty. On their tenth anniversary Giovanni was hired by the State of Oregon to take over their newly formed petty crime division in Ashland, Oregon. Their third child, Antonio, was born there.

It was not too much later that Giovanni was named assistant Chief of Police which meant he was in charge of every difficult crime that was perpetrated in Ashland.

Giovanni was one tough cop and a much tougher father. There was only one edict that his son, Antonio, had to abide by. You study and study and then study some more and when you think you are one smart guy you go back and study some more. Giovanni's belief in Antonio was far surpassed by how much his son adored his father.

The town's small college was the pride of Ashland and Antonio's residence for four years. He proved to be an excellent student who graduated with a post graduate scholarship and an invitation to further his studies at Harvard with its largest scholarship.

Two years later he shocked his fellow Harvard graduates with the pronouncement that he was heading back to Ashland.

They screamed back, "You are doing what?"

"Yes, I'm going back to the city I love and back to the people I adore. I'm going home."

Their unanimous retort to that stupidity was that he must have suffered a mental breakdown and they would give him a year or two before he was back in some big city fighting to make up for the loss of time he had permitted himself in his silly adventure back home.

Despite their laughter he did return to Ashland. He knew where his heart lay, and he was soon hired by the most influential bank in Ashland.

His work focused on the economics of a small city like Ashland and how to increase the funds that found their way into, and stayed in said town. Each year at least one new corporation opened or expanded their growth in Ashland.

Almost two years to the day after his return to Ashland his father had been promoted to leading a department against the drug pushers in all of Southern Oregon. They did not have a big force but they were more than diligent in every part of their efforts.

A great deal of investigative work had been done over almost one full year. His father and several dozen officers were prepared to strike their foremost target. They knew where the villains were and how much drugs they had in their possession. The raid was made late one evening when all was pitch black.

Captain D'Angelo had his men cover all sides of the house that they knew was headquarters for this gang. At the given word they charged the house with rifles blazing away. No fire was returned. It was a huge success as some nine men were captured as well as tons of banned drugs.

The good Captain D'Angelo made one mistake.

He saw to it that all the prisoners were cuffed and tied into the squad cars. He and his lieutenant then walked through the house to make certain that was there were no drugs left behind.

The house was bare. Nothing was hidden anywhere in the house or cellar. As he and his fellow officer turned away a closet door opened ever so slightly. Behind the crack in the door and hidden beneath a pile of old blankets a wounded criminal raised a rifle and fired two shots. Giovanni and his aide were instantly killed.

Antonio had just reached his parent's home where his mother had prepared some real Italian food that could feed an army. The meal was its usual success. Antonio and his mother were, per usual, cleaning up all in the dining room and kitchen when they heard a soft knocking on the front door. Antonio's mother opened the door and took but one look at the men standing there, all with their hats in their hands. Their faces were of the saddest she had ever seen.

Not a word was spoken before she started screaming. Her screams were answered with tears pouring down all of the officers' faces.

Antonio arrived at the door just in time to catch his mother as she started falling to the floor. His mother fainted away and, truth to say, she never recovered from hearing the dire words that were ultimately spoken to her.

Within a month, she and her youngest daughter had moved to New York City and the home of her eldest son. She had to flee from Ashland and the curse that had enveloped them.

Antonio was far too damaged to even think of leaving the grave site of his father.

The man who had tutored him about all the good in the world was no longer available to him. He couldn't stop crying nor could he find one solitary reason to continue living.

Alcohol became the one crutch he could rely on. First

it was a drink or two at night. This seemed to work as he started laughing about things. A swig or two before taking off for the office each morning was easy to hide. And the alcohol seemed to drive the tears away.

Two months later he was fired from the bank. One night he was going through a batch of letters his father had sent him while he was at Harvard. Each letter contained essentially the same closing lines.

"Never forget who you are. Don't look for the easy way out of the problems you will certainly face. I never did. You are a far better man than I ever dreamt I could be. I kiss you. I love you."

After some time those words became his mantra. He slowly cut down on his drinking. Then one day he resolved to end drinking any fluid stronger than Coca Cola.

He was in his late twenties when he lost his father. It took him many years to regain complete stability. He never regained his passion for work but found peace and refuge in his now long held job as grounds' custodian in this wonderful cemetery.

Chapter Sixteen

$\mathcal{A}$shland challenged both Rich and Tim as soon as they made it their home. Perhaps it was more the two boys daring the town to allow them to get to know each and every path outward, away, and most importantly back to the building they lived in.

They were standing in front of their new home as Rich was about to challenge Tim.

"Tim, my fine lad, today you get your first chance to go it alone. I want you to take your first solo trip to any part of town that you would like to visit. But whenever you get to that place I want you to turn around and come on home. Remember that the most important part of the trip is getting home."

What he did not tell his brother was that should he get lost Rich would have been following him from the very first and would be there to pick him up if necessary.

"Rich I can't do that."

"Sure you can. Just tell yourself you can do it and you will succeed. I believe in you and you have never let me down so get going right now."

Timothy took one last look at his brother. The thought of being all alone outdoors was as scary as could be. He stared long and hard down the street as he sucked in his breath and then, ever so slowly, started walking away from Rich.

At first his pace was beyond slow, but bit by bit he started walking faster. He soon became more interested in looking at all the store windows than in completing his mission. He was having such a fine time that he forgot his initial idea of where he would walk to. Strangely enough it didn't bother him one whit. He paused and stared up at the sky and then shouted out loud that he knew where he was.

"This is where those nice kids play the guitar and sing those great songs."

He was somewhat uncertain about exactly where he was but he felt he was headed in the right direction.

Remembering his mission, he stepped up his pace. He went about five blocks more before he realized that he was not going home. He stopped. He was the slightest bit frightened. He looked in all directions and then he recalled being next to that large metal fence that blocked off a place where a new house was being built.

He spun around delighted with himself, as he was certain that he knew just where he was. He kept walking directly into the heart of Ashland. He smiled at how far he had gotten. All the way he kept whispering to himself about how smart he was. A huge smile creased his face.

Right ahead was the big theatre where Rich sometimes worked. Behind it was the outdoor theatre and beyond it the wonderful park with hundreds of beautiful trees always singing out their songs. To him it was the most peaceful place he had ever seen.

Rich, who had silently and nervously been following his brother kept back from Tim while wondering if his brother knew he was now not too far from home.

Tim just kept looking from one tree to another. For the first time in his life he had crossed several unknown streets by himself. He knew what he had accomplished and was proud of what he had done.

Rich chuckled with pride as he watched Tim hug and then kiss one tree after the other. He was certain that Tim was also smiling.

Tim next stepped back from this brace of trees, once again hugged another tree, shook his head and turned backwards towards home.

Rich was certain that Tim was smiling as he had to pick up his pace to match that of Tim's. He short cut his way home so as to beat Tim there.

Some twenty minutes later Tim entered their building where he was greeted by Rich loudly shouting "Congratulations, Tim. I'm proud of you my man."

A quick hug of Tim and then Rich proclaimed that since today was Monday, which meant no show today, they were going to celebrate Tim's sweeping through all those streets by having dinner at the great pizzeria in town. Be it New York or Ashland, pizza was their favorite dish.

"Rich, can I first ask you a question. How come you always show up to meet me, and that's even when I don't know where I am?"

"Like I've always told you wherever you are I am also there so you never have to worry about anything."

"Rich, Rich. I believe you. That's why I was having such a good time. I wasn't scared at all. I just wanted to get to these trees and smell them."

"Is there anyone that you would like to join us?"

"Yes, yes, yes. Let's take Tony."

"That's a great idea! And just who is this Tony?"

"Oh, Tony is a new friend of mine."

"And where did you meet this Tony?"

"I think it was at the park across the street from here."

Ever fearful for his little brother, Rich probed on. "That park is really a cemetery."

"Oh yes. Tony told me all about cemeteries but I forget. What's a cemetery?"

"I'll tell you all about that later but Tony sounds interesting, so tell me more about Tony."

"Oh, he is just a nice guy who works in the park or the seminary."

Rich interrupted his brother, "No, it is called a cemetery."

"Okay, cemetery. That's where we met. Yeah, Tony told me all about cemeteries. Would you like me to show you where I met Tony?"

"That sounds great to me."

With that Tim grabbed Rich's arm and raced him into the adjacent cemetery. Within minutes they stood facing a particular gravestone.

"This is where Dr. Rountree lives. It's where I met Tony."

With that Tim took Rich's arm and led him closer to the stone he had pointed out.

"Tony told me all about Dr. Rountree and he also told me all about cemeteries and a lot of other things. It was fun talking to him."

"Right again, Bro. Hey, I bet you I can beat you home."

With that Rich started racing off with Tim right behind him.

They passed few people as they raced out to the street that hugged the cemetery but, when they did pass some pedestrians, they broke into laughter at the strange looks that broke out on the faces of those people who couldn't or wouldn't comprehend why anyone would be running madly through these very peaceful grounds.

Those people would stare after Rich and Tim with puzzled looks as they wondered what drove on this obviously mad twosome.

The two young men espied the puzzled looks that greeted them from the people they passed and their laughter grew as they saw odd grimaces that seemed to burst forth on the faces of all they flew by.

Chapter Seventeen

By nine o'clock the next morning both brothers were again pacing up and down at the spot where Tony and Tim had met.

Tony spied them from the other end of the Cemetery. He wondered what they were doing there so early in the morning but he had to finish replanting a new Maple Tree that had somehow caught a wind that spun it halfway to the ground.

He shouted out to them that he would soon be finished with this job. He jumped up and down. Neither Tim nor Rich looked his way. Tony was as annoyed as could be. He threw his shovel to the ground and stormed up to where the boys stood. He was not in the mood for pleasantries.

"You guys must be deaf. I've been shouting at you like crazy but you just didn't turn my way no matter what I did. I've got a half fallen tree down there that I should be replanting right now."

Rich apologized. He said that it was his fault they had

been so distracted from where Tony had been. With it came his offer to help with what Tony was currently working on.

Tony roughly agreed that another hand could help in his chore. A brief walk back to the Maple and within fifteen minutes of joint effort the task was done.

As soon as the tree was solidly planted Tony took them back to Dr. Rountree's grave. The flow of talk and the obvious efforts of the boys to please turned a mere relationship into a budding friendship.

"As you can see there are many good souls who are buried in graves here."

"You see Rich. That is what Tony was trying to tell me about yesterday. I didn't understand him then and I still don't understand a word he says. What are good souls and what is burying and graves?"

Rich jumped in with the fact that good souls are nice people who are kind to everyone. Sometimes they get tired and they retire from the normal world and live in what is called graves and are liked by everyone for their kindness and gentleness. Rich added that burying means placing someone in a spot that they are comfortable in.

"Do we know any good souls?"

"Sure. You are a good soul and so is Tony."

"Why are we good?

Tony, with a huge smile on his face, answered, "Because we are afraid of being bad."

This broke up Tim and Rich who guffawed at the silliness of the reply. Tim joined in even though he didn't have a clue as to why he was laughing but he accepted that answer for he feared any further explanations would leave him even more confused.

"I'm sorry, Tim. Just forget yesterday and anything I said then. I watched you standing at Dr. Rountree's grave and I wondered why you picked out that stone but you sure picked a winner. He is a wonderful man. This whole place is for people who reach an age where they go to sleep. Their friends find a comfortable place for them to rest in and they usually spend all their time relaxing there.

Tim asked what was written on the stone resting atop the grave, and why did all the stones have different words atop them.

"That's simple enough. Just as we do, they have an address atop their stone and it tells the world where they live. They spend most of their days fast asleep.

Tim queried, "And do they ever wake up again?"

"Maybe, but I don't know if anyone has ever chosen to do so. It is such a nice place that I can't see why one would want to leave it. Everyone who goes to his or her grave is in what we affectionately call 'going to perpetual sleep.'"

"I like to sleep. When will I take that sleep?"

"Not for many, many years. The most important thing to know is that we love the people who are sleeping here and they love us."

"Well, why don't we wake them up and tell them how much we love them"

"They know that, and they will tell us when they want to wake up."

Tony realized that the conversation was getting a bit too complex for Tim and switched to a summation of that talk.

"Well congrats to all of us for doing such a great job on replanting that tree."

Tim asked if that was all Tony did to keep everything so beautiful.

With a hearty laugh, Tony told of having to take care of a few other things like keeping all these graves so that the people who were sleeping there were never disturbed.

Tim then popped out at Tony, "Promise me that someday you will tell us all about you and your work."

"Tim, I'm really just an old dummy, and it won't be too long until you will know everything about me. But first could you do me a favor? I left my best shovel at the foot of the Maple Tree. I wouldn't want just anybody to pick it up. Could you run up there and get it?"

Tony had purposely left the shovel at the tree near his cabin so that he could get some time alone with Rich.

Rich urged Tim to show Tony how fast he could run up there and get the shovel. "I expect you to break all records both on the run up there and on the way back."

Tim barely heard the words as he flew away from Tony and Rich. He was soon halfway up the hill which got Rich laughing as he told Tony he guaranteed Tim would be smelling the trees on the way back so they would have more than enough time to talk.

"When he gets back, just jump into the life of Michael Rountree and don't get into anything sordid about the man. Tim is the sweetest kid you will ever meet but he has a strange malady that is elusive of any cure. If you keep everything simple you wouldn't know anything was wrong with him. So keep it at a level that he can handle and you'll find him to be a total delight."

Chapter Eighteen

The talk between Rich and Tony was quite short. It did not take Rich too long to spell out all of Tim's problems, nor did it take any time at all for Tony to empathize with both brothers.

Rich laid out the ailments Tim suffered from but stressed about how great and well-being a kid he was.

"I love him very much and he brings me much joy. I try to keep things short and simple for him. It isn't easy to differentiate for him what is good and what is bad and eventually he, in his own way, gets the message. Keep everything you tell him at a simple level and I assure you he will be right there with you."

The more difficult part to explain was what they had learned in the doctor's office.

"Doctors have said he has Asperger's Syndrome which means he sometimes has troubles in talking to other people and many physical things can bewilder him. He would love to have friends, but his peers often see him as odd and an easy target for bullying and teasing. He does have mood dis-orders but on the other hand he is as sweet as can be most of the time. Though to be totally honest with you, he does have severe depression at times and other times will go off on a temper tantrum. Fortunately, he hasn't had a one since our moving out here."

"Hold it, Rich. I get the picture. In the little time I know him, he has come across as a sweet and genuine good boy. It's easy to see the problems, but it is just as easy to see what a great kid he can be. Rich, I promise you Tim and I will have a fine time together. That brother of yours is a treasure and I hope you trust me enough to allow me to be a real friend to both of you."

Rich thankfully replied that it would be a delight for both Tim and himself to honor such a friendship.

"In fact let me tell you of what I have embarked on and you will be the only one I tell of it."

He then went on to tell of his feeling that the time had come to get Tim into doing something of purpose.

Once again, Tony jumped in with, "That's a great idea but make sure that Tim thinks it is an important job and is something that he will take great pride in doing."

"Well, yesterday afternoon I met with Marilyn Lange. She is the head of the theatres off-stage activities. I told her of Tim's problems and that I was certain that Tim and I will be great at whatever she asks us to do. When she heard that both of us would work together on whatever she came up with she immediately offered us the most important task that was still open."

Rich laughed as he told Tony that Marilyn said there was only one opening left at the Festival and it was a rather demeaning one.

"She started telling us that it was ours if we cared to take it, even though it wasn't the nicest work, but I cut her off by instantly shouting 'We'll take it.' "

He then went on describing the job and how it involves their cleaning the Bowmer Theatre's bathrooms after each matinee and evening show.

"I didn't listen to any of her put-downs of the job. Since it was the only job being offered and, coincidentally, fell right into our requirement that it be a very important job. I knew it was made for Tim and me. She called it menial but it was a real job to us and a paying one at that so I couldn't have cared less about hearing that it was a menial job. It was the first job of Tim's life, and it was important because Marilyn Lange entrusted us to do a job that would be judged everyday by their most valued customers, the ever complaining theater goers."

Within moments, Tim returned with shovel in hand and a smile on his face and shouting about how much fun he had doing his work for Tony.

Tony's only comment was "Well done, lad, you are a great worker. That is just as I would have handled it."

That evening the new job was performed as if it was a scientific experiment. Rich and Tim were meticulous in their attacking every spot in each bathroom. They were both as exhausted as could be but equally elated. Tim just glowed with what they had done.

Tim felt good about himself when somebody expressed their praise for him being hired by Marilyn for this job. It was the finest complement Tim had ever received.

Chapter Nineteen

The three men were in a deep discussion about what kept Tony most busy when, out of the blue, Tim asked the others if they knew that one could tell which tree is which by smelling it?

A brief argument broke out between Rich and Tim about the veracity of that statement.

Tony joined into the conversation by declaring he didn't have any free time to argue about this nonsense.

"So let's get right to it and forget about the trees. I agree with you and smelling the damned trees."

Puzzled, Tim exclaimed that he had never heard of a Damned Tree and wondered what other species it belonged to.

Tony answered that it was a very rare species and quickly went on with his description of the words on that stone.

"The lettering on each stone identifies who is the resident of that resting spot. The stone you like so much is for Doctor Michael Rountree. He was the first doctor who had come with his wife to live in Ashland. Goodness knows all the folks living in Ashland those early days needed his help."

Tim broke in again by asking when the good doctor got to Ashland.

"Good question, Tim. He and his wife, Annette, first came to Ashland early in 1856. That's a long time ago. She was a ton younger than him, but they sure were a loving pair. She was as pretty as can be and smarter by a mile than all of us put together."

"Thanks, Tony, but I have another great question. Could you slow down a bit and tell me how you got all that information about Dr. Rountree?"

"Well, for one thing, a book about Ashland was written some time ago. It includes a lot about the good doctor and his wife. I've read that book at least three times and I've just about memorized it. The second thing is that he was such an important man in Ashland that people would be writing stories in the local paper for years and years about the exploits of our Dr. Rountree."

He continued with more verbiage about where Michael was born and Michael's family.

"Michael was born in England the fourth of three prior born sisters. His proud father, finally siring a male, eagerly wanted the boy to be named after himself but was vetoed by his much stronger wife. It was her beloved father who received the honor of having the new grandson named after him. The grandfather was much better known throughout southern England.

Shortly after Michael's birth, his father passed away and left their somewhat prosperous accounting business to

Michael's mother. It was rare indeed that a woman would take over a business, but most of their clients were pleased with the change in management.

She, of course, did a far better job than her husband had done. She was a born money maker for her business and her clients.

As the boy grew, all who knew the family quickly realized that Michael possessed more of his mother's genes than the bland ways of his quiescent father.

The three sisters were fair-haired, pleasant and as dull as their father. Each day Michael demonstrated to all that this young boy was the gifted one. That he was the star of the family was quickly recognized and accepted by all.

Tim was glued to every word Tony uttered. His mouth was agape while his eyes were constantly darting between Rich and Tony. Much of what was being said he did not understand but the trees were beautiful and the fact that these two adults were including him in their discussion was pure joy to him. He could have sat there forever and never uttered a word nor understood much of what was being said, yet still be in pig heaven.

Tony continued with how Michael's mother adored her very tall son as did his three sisters. They looked up to him both for his height but also for his brains. He didn't give a hoot about any of them.

They had no idea as to how outrageous he would become. They were peaceful and content with the quiet life of Kent. He rallied against it from the very first. Something within him pushed for more. He wanted more, no, he demanded more.

Young Michael breezed through the English schooling system and became the smartest in all his classes. He soared through the Early Foundation Stage (3-5 years), devastated primary education (6-11) and blazed through secondary stage (12-18). Throughout all his schooling, he was by far the best scholar as well as the strongest athlete in whatever school he was attending.

By his 18th year he was quickly enrolled in medical school. Soon after starting at the finest med school in all of England, he decided that being a doctor might eventually cover his financial needs but would only satisfy a small part of his real life.

He deplored the dullness of all the other English gentlemen he encountered and was bored by his family. He dreamt only of adventure and new discoveries. As a young man he cast scorn on what was normal in England and, as he grew, America and stories of the riches known to be almost pouring out of the earth there excited him

He had no desire to have a girlfriend nor, for that matter, did he need a chap to pal around with. What Michael demanded of himself was that he must be successful in whatever he attempted. Conquering all was of infinite importance. What Michael wanted, Michael obtained. It mattered not that littered bodies were strewn over every path he took.

What was most puzzling about Michael Rountree was that he had no rationale for even thinking about leaving his home in England. He easily become a busy doctor and his financial adventures were almost always successful. To say the least, he was a most complex man. The words of fortunes being made in the United States became too tempting for him to ignore.

After much thought, in 1850 the exciting reports of the booming financial times in America awakened him to the need for him to join those battles. He sold his medical practice and then sold everything of value which included everything he owned in Kent.

He soon left England and never returned to home and family.

He arrived in New York and immediately set off gathering acquaintances with anyone who was not native born in the U.S. He was glib and could be a good listener. Where and how they had succeeded was of great importance but where they had failed was possibly of greater import. What his new friends were not aware of was that this charming and erudite young chap was testing each of them for some future use.

It was a quick and effective way of acquiring tools from those which could aid him in answering his need to be successful. The best of this adventure led to his meeting a fascinating and quite attractive young woman, Annette Devalais.

Though having been born in France, she had resided in New York since she was five years old. He was thirty five years old while she was not quite twenty when they first met.

What attracted her to this much older man was that she had the same yearnings for a different life as he did. Annette was Michael's intellectual equivalent and, of greater import, she had an evil streak in her body that pushed her far beyond what his limitations were. They both quickly learned that neither of them had any worries about taking advantage of the weaknesses of others.

Her parents did all they could to separate this pairing,

but within two years they were married. They were never to give birth to any children.

Michael was the first to clearly recognize that Annette was by far the more adventuresome of the two. She was the first to bring the idea of California into their discussions. He recognized that she was on target with setting the west coast as their first area to explore.

With equal speed and abandon, this unusual couple set out to meet the challenge that California gold sent out to the world. If anyone could succeed in having the gold come their way it was this unique pair. At the end of their first year of marriage, their plans to attack California were complete. Late in 1855 they excitingly set off to conquer the West Coast. Their arrival in southern California proved to be exactly one year too late as the days of fortunes pouring out of California Rivers had slowly faded away.

They soon realized that there was too little gold and very little room for them to make any headway against the already established and power crazed entrepreneurs who had stripped or corralled the wealth of the state.

A brief stay in northern California led to less than limited success. Then they heard words of excitement about small strike after small strike in southern Oregon. The words booming southward was instrumental in leading the Rountree family north.

They yearned for exciting real estate adventures and means of building their funds in more non-traditional manners. It was not much longer when the Rountree couple arrived in the quaint little town of Ashland Mills, Oregon.

This town had first been settled many, many years ago by Takelma and Shasta Indians. The white man and his guns began to control the area covering Ashland Mills and its surrounding territory.

Yes, it seemed a foregone conclusion that the Indian would be driven from his home land but it quickly became a day to day battle that raged for years on. Slowly the white man began to win battle after battle.

The rapidly growing town promised all sorts of involvements that could lead to attaining great financial success. The Rountrees arrived in Ashland Mills just a bit after the harrowing battles with the Indian was starting to peter out.

Early on, the greatest danger to voyagers coming north was the dangerous fact that they were invading a territory heavily populated with Takelma and Shasta Indians. Soon these tribes were joined by several other Indian groups who brought with them an even greater hatred of the pale faces that had invaded this land they clung to.

In normal days they fought one another, but the advent of a new enemy, the white man, united them into an almost ceaseless warfare against this far more aggressive enemy.

There is little doubt but that the Indians were the initiators of the first battles between themselves and the ever growing masses of white men. The attacks on these newcomers was not to kill them but to advise them that this had been the red man's land for centuries and they intended to keep it that way.

The first Indian versus the invading white man battle led to three white men being mercilessly slaughtered and their bodies left to float in a nearby stream. The Indians had swept in while the white men were panning for gold. Totally preoccupied with their task, the battle lasted but minutes and war was officially declared.

The word of these deaths spread quickly but nothing dissuaded the men who were driven by the thought of gold coming their way.

All dangers were ignored. Each passing day elevated the conflict between the two combatants. The white man's refusal to recognize the Indians as human beings brought forth major deaths on both sides.

The immigrants migrating into this northern territory could not waste time placating these wild and unintelligent natives. They were here to find gold and not to satisfy these crazed Indians.

The battles became fiercer and fiercer, but the original owners of these lands were at a disadvantage. The rifles owned by the intruders were far more lethal than the bow and arrow possessed by the lands' original owner. The battle all but ceased within a few years. The conquest of the white man over the Indian allowed the victors to more quickly embrace and develop this beautiful area.

They could build their town while pulling up gold. Yes, panning for gold and building a town kept things humming for all.

The Rountrees, in their research of the town, found much to like about the tiny village. But most of all they loved the fact that there was no doctor in residence and sufficient other financial doings to interest both of them. The city seemed just perfect in the eyes of Michael and Annette.

The two did not know a soul in this lovely village, nor what was in store for them when they first landed there, but they were certain that this would be their world to conquer. It did not take too long for them to set upon a path that would lead them to grand economic success and then a horrendous defeat.

Michael Rountree's favorite saying was, "We English folk once lost America but we Rountree's are here to take it back." They quickly purchased a home that had been built by a young couple who had lost their taste for the difficulties they faced in this new town.

The Rountrees offer for the house was more than generous and therefore impossible to refuse. Within days after the new owners occupied their new residence, a note of their arrival in town was sent out to all the important people in town asking them to come to join the Rountree family at a gala party they were throwing.

Chapter Twenty

Tim could hardly wait for the next scheduled meeting with Tony but, truth would tell, he never fully comprehended what the man was saying. Nevertheless, he pushed his brother to set another meeting with Tony. As always, Rich immediately contacted Tony and an early meeting was set for the following morning,

Tony went out of his way as he prepared for their meeting with much hot coffee and six large and delicious biscuits. Obviously he was enjoying their meetings as much as the boys were.

"Well, nice of you boys to show up. I was about to eat all this great grub I made myself. A full stomach always assures me of a good time so let's all dig in and the verbiage will soon be flowing from all of us."

Within moments of finishing the last biscuit, Tony started out on the lecture of the day.

"Since there are no fallen trees to distract us, I've decided to get right into a rather serious matter."

Tony was having the time of his life. He could not have been a happier man than in leading these discussions with his new found friends. He loved being the professor to these two ever grateful students. What he had never told them was the fact that he had earned a master's degree in economics.

"I got to thinking last night about you two and what you don't know about this sweet little city. What it was and what it is today are so different. Now we are filled with a bunch of pseudo intellectuals who are mostly roaring liberals. In the early days there was only one thing that drew people here and that was gold. This little town was occupied by folks from all over America, though a majority seemed to be from the east coast and, in particular, the State of Kentucky."

The boys were hooked. Food was forgotten as Tony's words had them enraptured.

"By 1852 word had reached out about the almost complete demise of the gold rush in California. At the same time gold was beginning to show its face in Oregon, so more and more folk headed there. The strikes were hardly in the numbers of central California but gave promise of returns that urged many a family to leave California and transfer their loyalties to Oregon."

Tony went on in detail about family after family arriving in Oregon driven there by a common greed to become wealthy. Few achieved that status. They prayed that their fortune would come easily but most ended up poorer than when they first reached Oregon.

As a good doctor, Rountree concentrated on his practice and on the financial side helping those in need of dollars to continue their digging for gold. Between his ever growing practice, his wife's thriving jewelry trade and his knee-deep involvement in the many financial deals that were constantly worked in this naïve little city, his wealth was growing rapidly.

Tony kept staring at the brothers and saw the bewilderment that was coursing through both faces. He was enjoying every second of haranguing the brothers and decided to really lay it on them. He switched from the Rountree's and launched into how difficult all was for the entire community.

Dreams had propelled hundreds of people to Oregon. For most of the new arrivals it was the gold that enticed them northward. Common talk amongst all of the gold diggers was that their next strike was sure to be the big one. Unfortunately very few made that strike.

At that point, Tony hit them with a new analogy.

"You know something, you guys are just like the original settlers out here. They came here to find gold that would assure them of having a fine life. You came here to find a different kind of gold but one that would bring you the assurance of a moneyed and pleasant life. The smart ones of those days played it real safe with their gold while you are constantly striving to be a better actor than the next guy so that you will get the better parts and larger salaries than the guy you top."

Rich tried to counter these words but the more he heard them the more he accepted the truth of what Tony had offered them.

Tony next presented the thought that as the population increased in those days, it became apparent that if

Ashland Mills was to succeed there were two needs that had to be addressed.

First, they must have a saw mill built. This would promote the ease of building better homes and make life a bit easier. Two of the wealthiest men in town had that mill built. It made them yet another fortune.

In the same manner, a water mill was completed almost on the very same day. The third and fourth additions to town were a church and a small school. In tribute to these important accomplishments, the name of the city officially became Ashland Mills.

The total package added up to the realization that Ashland Mills was a wonderful place to live in, but the desperate search for gold was a daily debilitating battle. Only a few of the bravest could sustain the battle. Hordes found this was too hard a war. Each day yet another family conceded defeat and stole back to their original home.

Ashland Mills had provided very little gold and equally little security. Those who stayed found little cash coming to them but a way of life that brought much pleasure. Stay they did, with the faith that this city would somehow bring them joy, if not financial success.

As the town slowly grew, another source of wealth raised its treacherous head. It was certainly of more evil substance. 'Commerce' was its name.

Who owned what, and why one house was worth more than the one next door was an enigma. Only a few were willing to gamble their fortunes in this almost daily warfare. A select group of men controlled more and more of the town.

It was this grouping that Michael Rountree started competing with, and his wins were far more often than his failures. Who would be of greater importance emerged as a constant war.

Finding gold required cash to back the physical efforts in the digging for same. It, in turn, brought out vile hostility between the haves and the almost haves. Of course, this effort allowed those interested in public office to bring their rivalry into a dreadful rivalry that shocked and divided the town.

The Rountrees became very involved in those melees. They seemed to triumph in most of those wars but, unfortunately, fate spun a different course for them.

Ashland Mills, to a large number of families, remained a delight. Both men and women early on fell in love with the fact that the climate was amazingly temperate. Fruits of all kinds abounded in all of the area. Luscious peaches and brilliant pears and strawberries vied with delicious blackberries for all. One could live with just the fruit which was ever at hand.

Winters, on the other hand, could be quite dire whereas Spring and Summer delighted all.

The women living in Ashland Mills were the real settlers. They were the ones who saw the possibility of claiming something more valuable than gold. To them living in Ashland Mills was almost idyllic.

The town slowly grew and with it a pride emerged that applauded the people who stayed. Together they had built a way to sustain themselves and they were increasingly heard to talk of 'The Town We Built.'

The Indian Tribes had settled here long before the white man had any thoughts of this land. They cherished their homeland whereas the white man worshipped only the gold that abounded in the waterways of Oregon. What mattered now was the ability of the white man to draw much in gold from the waters of the area.

The summer of 1850 was ablaze with battle after battle between the invaders and the natives. The weaponry became overwhelmingly favorable to the white man as bows and arrows were not at all equal to rifles.

Word spread from tribe to tribe that 'The only good white man was a dead white man.' In contrast, the white men screamed the equally absurd maxim 'Never trust a red face.' Both sayings led to blood being constantly spilled on both sides.

However, if one honestly compared the rationale for each side, the Indian could be seen as trying to save their land whereas the intruders were merely trying to enrich themselves by stealing gold from the streams. It mattered not how difficult it was to battle the Indians or the fact that panning for gold in the local streams became less and less rewarding. This was their land and there was no way they would be turning east again.

Yes, gold was far less plentiful and slowly disappeared entirely, but the uniqueness of the city they were building made living there all the more wonderful.

Tony let it all sink in and then took a deep breath. He softly told his students that there was still a great deal to tell, but it was too late to continue now. He left them with one sentence that intrigued them.

"Far worse came to the city years later when the KKK came here to spread its hatred. It was hatred that nearly destroyed this town."

Tim rather ferociously shouted out "Tony, Tony, what is a KKK."

"Just hold on Tim and you'll soon find out all you'll want to know about the KKK."

Chapter Twenty-One

$\mathcal{T}$ony was most anxious to bring his class up to date on the story of early Ashland, for there was also great interest in the more modern days.

Two days later, Tony nodded to the class and then jumped right into a new story about Michael and Annette.

"Now just about everyone in town were more than joyous about the fact that finally a physician had settled in Ashland Hills. The women of the town of course idolized Michael, and Annette was simply adored by all."

Tony told of the Rountrees quickly making new friends aware of their financial prowess, which brought forth dire fury within the current economic leaders of the town. Michael's battles with some of the more interesting economic activities of his opponents explained a lot about their antipathy towards him.

Michael went out of his way in proving to all that he had the knowledge and fervor to be a winner. Primarily, this involved the purchasing of mineral rights, which meant gold, and properties, which meant housing.

Yes, there was no huge open-armed greeting of the Rountrees by the financiers who controlled Ashland, but this was counter balanced by the delighted thanks bestowed on them by every patient the doctor had, be it with words or homemade food specialties that were made as a special gift for 'the wonderful new couple that had just come to their town,' or the kind words of delight expressed to them by just about everyone they met.

A quaint three story log house had recently been built by a newlywed couple named Webber. It had taken most of their finances and efforts to erect said structure. Their failure in amassing any gold led to their need to sell the house.

The availability of the building and the arrival of the Rountrees was a blessing for the seller and buyer. What started out as a rental negotiation in short order became a purchasing debate. When the price reached the point where the Webbers could return to Ohio with a handsome amount of money in their pockets, the deal was consummated.

Several folks in town competed with the Rountrees for the purchase of the house but the swiftness of the negotiation and the amount of money involved in the purchase rapidly cut out all but the Rountrees. It also added many more of the important families in town to the list of violent anti-Rountree believers.

The building itself was as plain as could be. The first floor was split between one large room which became the doctor's reception area and a smaller room which served as his examination room. Two other small rooms provided the space for Annette's unique boutique.

The entire second floor became the residence for the Rountrees. It featured a living room, dining room, enormous kitchen, with a large bedroom and bath.

The Rountrees added an outside staircase which led to the third floor which held five bedrooms and one small toilet. It became the sole hotel in town. A goodly number of the 'for hire gold miners' found it less expensive when two shared a single room.

There is no doubt but that this town was controlled by some very tough men. Nevertheless, the Rountrees were adored by the women who fought off their husband's orders to just wait and see who these Rountrees were before welcoming them into the inner circles of the town. The women relished having the doctor and his wife to gossip about. They giggled about how very handsome he was, and wasn't her French accent delightful.

The beauty and sweetness of Annette raised almost perpetual gossip amongst Ashland's women. Her unusual collection of rare and expensive items, which she had bought with her, was a constant temptation for purchase. A flow of new goods from France and England kept her shelves replete with unique examples of what these women had been forced to leave behind when they set off to this new world.

Her delicious French words which flowed in and out of her dialogue and her beauty was a constant draw to both men and women.

The men reacted to Annette, while spending an inordinate amount of time supposedly looking for something very special they were purchasing for their wives. It mattered little what said piece would cost, for Annette always assured them that each piece was offered at a 'most reasonable' price. They assured themselves that the something they would finally purchase was something they did only for their loved and long suffering wives.

Annette's beauty was the prime reason for the men losing all sense of what a golden piece, or any of her trinkets she offered for sale, was really worth what she was asking.

Annette also reduced the pain in each woman's heart. They all longed for that once loved picture or dish set given to them by their grandmother. Each item was left at home as being too heavy or too cumbersome to take on the trip west. There was never a price tag on the more expensive items, for Annette would always offer one price for the item, then allow her friend and customer to cut the cost to where it could not be resisted.

It made purchasing an item so much fun that buying at Annette's was always a celebration. Her customers walked away with a smile of great satisfaction written all over their faces. They would always know they had 'stolen' the piece that they just loved. Of course, the piece was still expensive but Annette had brought it down enough so that they could not do anything but purchase it.

Annette begged each purchaser to only tell of the original asking price to their friends which more than pleased the new owners.

The men reacted to the sweetness of Annette, while spending an inordinate amount of money and time looking for something that she would recommend for their wives. No sales pitch was needed to sell her goods. Each item sold gave the purchaser the opportunity to brag to her neighbors about what she or her husband had just picked up at Annette's. Within one year in Ashland, the Rountree's wealth had soared far over what they possessed on their arrival into this wondrous little town.

Chapter Twenty-Two

*I*t was but two days later that Tim began bugging Tony for more about old Ashland Mills.

"Sorry my good friend, but I've told you enough about those old days, but if you'd like to know the names of these trees that tower above us I'll have a shot at that."

"Wow. I sure would."

Tony instantly pointed to the thick strand of trees that stood not five feet away from them.

"These are called Madrone trees and since ancient days they have been known as healing trees. They always grew near beds of water. If the original settlers had a cold, they would come down to the local stream, dip a cloth into the water near the Madrones and then wash themselves with the cloth. Since then, science has proven that was hogwash, but the legend about the Madrones continued on and on."

"But, Tony, if it first worked, then why doesn't it work today?"

"Maybe it does. Hey, here is a thought. Let's try our own test. The next time you have a cold come down here and soak a kerchief real well in the water that runs near these trees. Then we can see for ourselves whether it works or not."

Tim turned to Rich asking, "Can I do that."

"You got it Buddy."

Tony reentered the conversation by saying, "Let me give you the names of four other trees that abound in these fields.

First, there is the Elk tree, and I will tell you a wonderful story about that tree. In return, I want you to go to the library and come up with stories about the Black Oaks that are native here and also the ever popular Maples and my favorite, the legendary Cyprus, which I think is the grandest one of all."

Rich hopped up quite excited.

"Wait a second. I know that story, but I don't have time to tell you about it. Let me just say that the story was written by Hans Christian Anderson who was a famous Danish writer. He was most famed for the fairy tales that he wrote. In 1845 he and his son wrote a tale about a Fir tree. It was a very sad story. There was a tree that wanted to do great things for the world, but all it could do was grow and grow and grow. But that's it for today."

"Rich, was the story he wrote really true?"

"No, Tim. As I said it was a tale written by a famed writer. Maybe after you do the research on the other trees, we can write our own fairy tale about those trees. But I'm busy this morning, so let's postpone the rest of that story until some other time."

Actually busy was an understatement for he was up to his ears with both performing his current shows and also rehearsing the two new shows he would be doing in the next season. Obviously, there was little time for his relating fairy tales.

The new shows Rich was involved in were as distinct as feasible from the shows he had played in the previous season. One of the shows posed a serious problem for both Rich and a rather beautiful young actress he was supposed to be having an affair with.

Valerie Crawford, who shared the stage with Rich, had berated the Morton brothers for not spending more time off stage with her.

"I work as hard as you do in that nothing show we are now doing, and I have kept secret the fact that Tim is my boyfriend. So how come I never get to see either of you for any other time than onstage?"

Tim looked first to Rich then to Valerie as if he was questioning whether or not he was indeed her boyfriend.

To appease her, the brothers checked with Tony to see if Valerie could be asked to join them at the next session of the 'what else happened to the Rountrees.'

Tony's reply came in the form of two questions. "Is she pretty and is she smart?"

Tim handled both answers.

"She is the prettiest, nicest, smartest girl in all of Ashland and she tells everyone that I am her boyfriend."

As a matter of fact, Rich had been more than excited by Valerie. There was something special about her that kept him quite agog. Not only was she a fine actress, but he was most impressed when he learned that she had received a Master's degree in Theatre from Yale.

Rich laughingly recalled the first offstage meeting he had with Valerie.

"When I first heard of her going to Yale I made a big deal of her going there but she just laughed at me. She told me that her parents had first met when they both attended Yale. She wanted to leave it there, but I pressed her about her families going to that highbrow school."

Tim jumped in with the news that Val had written at least one book and ended his thoughts on the matter by saying, "Bring her on."

Before Tony could spit out an answer, Rich added additional information about the young lady.

"Valerie will confuse you with her looks. She is rather dark skinned and you might think that she is of the black persuasion. But if you look more closely you will be positive she is white. The answer to it all is her complex heritage. You see her father is a light skinned black man and her mother is white. Oh yes, they had met at Yale which each were attending. You might also want to know that her dad is Chief of Police in a big New York suburb and her Mom is the Principal of their local High School."

Tony rather angrily told Rich that he talked too much.

"You know, my friend, I couldn't care less if she was pink or chartreuse. As I recall, all I asked to know about her was whether she was pretty and smart. Your obviously biased words have me wondering whether you belong in this group"

Rich did not know the correct words to use in his apology to Tony but strongly replied that Tony would love her, and he added "She is one hell of a lot smarter than I am."

"Okay then. If she is as fine as you say she is and you spend this next week teaching her all you have learned about the early days of Ashland, you can bring her to our next get together."

Some two weeks passed before Tony could bring his new class together. Tony was more than pleased when Valerie appeared for the first time with the Morton brothers. She added a lovely radiance to his class which more than delighted him.

"First off, Valerie, you should know several things about this group of ours. You have a lot to learn about me and your fellow students. Their lack of intellect will at times dismay you, but I am very pleased as you are, obviously, a bright young woman. I have longed for a student with brain power so thanks for joining us. Tim here is as bright as they come but Rich is a dullard, so you'll have to accept the fact that we don't go too fast in this class."

Tim rushed to the defense of his brother saying he didn't know what the word dullard meant but he bet that Rich would know what it meant.

And if he doesn't, Valerie will definitely know it."

Valerie simply nodded her head and smiled. As a matter of fact she did very little talking throughout the entire session but now, as the lesson was about to end, she raised her hand and asked if she could add one sweet story she had read in a book about early Ashland. Tony readily agreed.

Valerie went on to tell them of a weekly event that Annette Rountree staged for the children who attended Ashland's little grammar school.

"One Friday morning, Annette came to the school and gave each student a small paper book. It was a simple French song book. Weekly, she would teach them one of the little songs included in the book. It was a tool she used to very gradually start teaching the class the French language. Annette rather quickly became the favorite teacher for all fifteen students.

Chapter Twenty-Three

Valerie, I'm glad that you know something of those new arrivals in town. Hopefully, Richard has brought you up to date on the Rountrees because that's what I am going to be talking about today."

At some length, Tony started detailing all he knew about the Rountrees.

"Yes, Michael was a bit of snob, but he directed that snobbery only towards those so-called town leaders who spent the bulk of their time garnering much money into their always open pockets."

Tony went on in some detail to tell of Michael and Annette welcoming the poorer folks in town with open arms. Yes, Doctor Rountree was much appreciated, as at last the locals had someone capable of fighting off those wearisome illnesses that made life such a burden. But they adored Annette because she was always so open to them and loved everyone she dealt with.

His medical fees were kept low for many an Ashland Mills resident. More than one family never received any billing for services received.

If your ailment was difficult and the patient had need of serious medical attention, it mattered not what you could pay or the length of time it took the patient to heal. Payment became a 'when you could afford to pay it' issue. The only thing of import was how long it took for the patient to recover from what disease they had been smitten with. All of his patients loved the wonderful doctor who made certain that they received the finest care feasible.

But there was one other side of the Rountrees that most people in Ashland loved. Annette's store was filled with the poshest goods that all in Ashland had ever seen. Very few of the common folk could afford any of the goods in her store but it was enough to look and dream of the day when one could buy something there. Those who could buy any of Annette's goods were certain to expose the item to all the other folk in town 'that mattered.'

However, what the upper class strongly resented most was the way the doctor and his wife ever constantly worked to become participants in all financial discussions bubbling in their town.

Many of the wealthy voices were also identified with the political leadership of the town. They worked hand in hand to shape the town, but were not appreciative of this doctor and his wife trying to include themselves in what made Ashland worthwhile.

The Rountrees however wielded one other strong card. They both possessed charm that was impossible to resist. The men of Ashland were bewitched by Annette. She was the woman every one of them lusted for. Michael's good looks and English accent captivated the women be they young chippies or older matrons.

Most of the antipathy leveled at the Rountrees grew out of the knowledge that this new twosome to Ashland was as bright if not brighter than they were. It further galled them that Dr. Michael was as keen a dealer in economic affairs as any of those who currently ran the city.

Truth be known, that group of men not only ran the city they owned the city.

Chapter Twenty-Four

*I*n his lectures about what Michael and Annette had to face in their Ashland early days, Tony stressed that most people in town were open armed about them. Some folk instantly loved them. Others tolerated them, and a small group of folk that controlled both the money and the politics of the town feared this doctor and his beautiful wife. Those folk were leery of anyone trying to break into their little cabal.

Michael was all too often driven by his singular commitment to ideas that could brighten the future of this city. Often he would tell Annette of an idea he had come up with and, unless she argued against said idea, he would proceed with making it a reality and a battle would ensue.

Even his thoughts on physical health was disparaged. One of his strongest thoughts dealt with making all the citizens of this wonderful new city physically healthy. Unfortunately, the more he preached and practiced his way to live one's life, the more those who had lived here for a longer time scoffed at his efforts.

The good doctor indulged in one self-centered practice each and every morning. He believed that exercising the body was the best medicine one could take to keep same healthy.

Unfortunately, most of the elite in town disbelieved anything Michael proposed and taught their fellow citizens that time spent resting in bed was the best medicine one could take.

Michael decided that just preaching about his road to good health would prove more effective if he did less talking about it and openly demonstrated it to his fellow citizens as a better way to go.

Thereafter each morning between 7:00 am to 8:00 a.m., he would open the back exit of his home. First he would pick up an obviously heavy bag of debris lying against his back wall. He would walk the debris bag to a huge container which sat some fifty yards into his field and dump the debris into same.

The next ten minutes would be occupied with stretches of every part of his body. This would be followed by a twenty to thirty minute jog which led him across the field that backed his property. The shortest run would carry him around the field at least three or four times. At other times the length of the jog would carry him across the field five or six times.

Everyone in town knew that the good doctor was demonstrating his way to health for the entire town.

He of course ignored the jibes he received for his jogging ritual, but each day he continued this ritual that he so loved.

It stirred great guffaws but he was delighted when a small coterie of youngish men began to emulate his ways. It was as if they had formed a secret society dedicated to walking their way to health.

Chapter Twenty-Five

Some two days later, Tony stared his lecture with words about a Christmas Sunday before Christmas, 1858. What was most notable was a lack of Christmas spirit flowing from those involved in several heatedly contested moneyed deals about to close.

Tony started detailing the story of that Christmas but Rich, fearing that this long verbal adventure might be boring to Tim, began a heated coughing fit aimed directly at Tony.

"Tony, if it's about that nude Thanksgiving Day party that really shook up this town then go ahead and tell us about it."

Tony picked right up on Rich's phony lead.

"Ah, Rich you've already blown the punch line for me. Besides that I have real work to do so get your asses out of here, and I'll see you tomorrow."

Valerie was the only one to protest against the stoppage.

It was three days later before Tony was once again ready to launch into a story that he felt was most import for his students to hear. Yes, the story was about Christmas but it was also about the truth of Doctor Michael Rountree's elimination from Ashland Mills.

It was a tale that had tortured most of the little city for years and years since that fatal day 1n 1858 when the good doctor was murdered.

Tony still felt that all but Tim should be told of the event that had laid such a curse upon Ashland. He, therefore, started with a little speech directed at his young friend.

"Hey, Tim, I've got to be honest with you. Today's lecture may be a little dull. It will probably be pretty boring to you. You can stay if you like, or you can join the crew down near the railroad tracks where they are going to be putting in a bunch of new trees."

Those words were a joy to Tim. Having a choice between listening to Tony spieling away or watching workers plant trees was simple. Tim cleverly advised Tony that the workers might need help with the trees, so he should get down to where they were working and tell them he was ready to help.

It took less than a few seconds before Tim was racing off to join the group who were hard at work planting the new trees.

Tony waited for Tim to disappear. What he was about to tell them focused on the death of Michael Rountree, and it was not a pleasant tale. The heart of the story was that Michael did not die pleasantly.

He had been murdered and the perpetrator of that monstrous crime was never discovered. It left all the residents of this quaint little town puzzled and ashamed of losing what most thought was one of the most important citizens of their little town.

Tony launched into his tale with the fact that "Despite the bitter cold morning, Michael Rountree emerged clad in his usual morning attire of thin pajamas and a bathrobe. He smiled when the cold first hit him and then did several self-created exercises. As the door behind him slid closed he spotted a group of five people who lived on the far side of his property. It was just a week before Christmas, and they were having a jolly time with a tree they had obviously just cut. The men were dragging a rather large Douglas Fir behind them.

Michael's neighbors then turned away from Michael so as to give them more traction with the tree. As they turned they noticed a lone figure coming out from a massive stretch of trees. He was crouching down as he bent and leaned towards the good doctor. For the life of them they could not recognize the man. They could see that he seemed to be carrying a large stick.

The unknown man began to kneel down and, at the same time, seemed to be pointing his stick at Doctor Rountree. Michael, ignoring the chap who was relatively close to him now, dropped his package of debris into the box that stood there. He rose and stared at the man now fully facing him."

Tony took a deep breath and hoped he was not about to make a great mistake in telling the remainder of this sad tale but he knew he had no alternative but to tell all.

"The young man of the Christmas tree group suddenly screamed out 'WHAT THE HELL. THAT'S A RIFLE HE'S CARRYING.'

He was pointing his hand towards the man he thought had been carrying a stick."

Tony paused again to let that thought be digested by Rich and Valerie. He looked from face to face of his class and when he had them further entranced with what would happen next he plowed ahead.

"Even Michael heard the words screamed out by the young fellow. He rose up and looked in the direction of the pointed hand. We don't know if Michael heard the rifle shot but we do know that a bullet hit him right in the chest. As they turned towards where the noise had come from they saw the man flying back into the woods."

Tony, ever so slowly began to force out further words.

"At the same moment, they witnessed the doctor rise, straighten up, and then collapse to the ground. The woman in the party started screaming while the oldest man of the group shouted out to his wife 'Mary take the kid and stay right here. Jim, you and Bob race down to where that fellow seemed to be. I'm going to see what happened to Michael.'

The four split off immediately. It took but a few moments for the older chap to reach Michael Rountree. There was no doubt but that the good doctor was no longer alive."

Tony paused for several moments to let that news sink in. Not a one stirred. They merely remained petrified, totally aghast as they tried to digest what they had just heard.

Tony didn't add a word preferring to let them stew over the horror he had just told them.

Much time passed ere he resumed telling the group of the young men speeding off towards where they had seen the man with the stick exit the field.

"But when they got to the spot where he was last seen, there was no sign of him anywhere. They next split up with one lad racing north through the woods while the other sped in the other direction. They tramped through every bit of ground in the woods and even out to the street that led to the treed area. Every direction was searched, but they found nothing more unusual than two large fresh piles of horse detritus with puffs of smoke still pouring out of both piles."

He went on to describe how they took different directions and frantically scoured the entire area looking for anything that might lead them to the missing man. Other than heavy footprints, nothing was found.

"But one sentence reached them all. It was their father shouting out 'Get down to the Sheriff's office and bring him back here right now."

He let many minutes speed by and it seemed as if he hadn't anything further to say.

Finally, Tony managed to speak the words that the father had shouted back to his wife. They were words that brought tears to all of Ashland. 'Michael has been killed and now you get over to Annette this very second.'

In response the woman rushed down to the Rountree house pulling her little girl as fast as she could. She found Annette in the kitchen preparing breakfast for her husband.

Tony could almost see the terror in the faces of Rich and Valerie. They had no words to offer but the message they had just been given shook them mightily.

After leaving some time to allow them to digest what he had said, Tony started again.

"Annette kept looking at her neighbor but couldn't seem to recognize a word she was saying. The woman knew she had finally reached Annette when the beautiful young woman gave out a pitiful moan and slowly sank to the floor. That day, Sunday, December 19th,

1858, was forever noted as the worst day that had ever hit Ashland Mills."

He then recounted that it took much time for Annette to realize that her life had just been shredded and that living without her man was too horrific to even consider.

It was not too long afterwards that Annette sold off all her holdings and returned to the east. No one in all of Ashland ever heard again from Annette Rountree.

For the first time, Rich took Val's hands and squeezed them tightly. The look on their faces was as if they did not want to hear another word, but Tony knew that there was still more to tell.

Almost silently Tony resumed his horrid report.

"A pall seized the entire city. Whether or not you personally knew the Rountrees, one had to know that an important part of the community was gone forever. The worst of it was the mystery of who had so viciously killed their Doctor. It was as if the entire town had conspired to murder that fine man."

Tony paused and looked at the two. It seemed as if they too were affected by the slaying of that good man. In as sad a voice as he could mutter he whispered, "And the craziest part of that entire horror was that the perpetrator of that killing has never been found."

The three of them just sat there without speaking a word. Rich and Val tried to ask a million questions but nothing came forth.

Quite a bit time passed before Tony could finish the story. He did so in muted tones that barely reached their ears. In those moments they learned that all the people of Ashland Mills mourned what had occurred that terrible day. Only one thought was shared by all. The killer must have been a hired hand of one of the town leaders who had lost a battle to Michael Rountree.

Rich stared at Tony then blurted out in astonishment, "Wait one bloody second. Are you trying to tell us that they never found the killer?"

"I didn't say no one knew who had done the killing or who hired who to do same. What I did say was that the killer went scot free because that's the way some people wanted it to be. It's been over one hundred years since that rueful day and still no one has come up with so much as a hint to who perpetrated that crime."

Chapter Twenty-Six

*V*alerie did not want the story of Rich and Tim becoming toilet cleaners to spread through the company. She feared that jokingly all the actors would use it to deride her men.

Nevertheless, word soon spread of the brothers' new-found job. However, rather than mocking them, the entire company, one by one, thought it was such a hoot that thereafter Tim and Rich's efforts in the toilets grew into a company effort.

Bit by bit actor after actor would turn up and the toilets would be clean in but moments. The only delay was caused by the almost constant laughter that roared through each bathroom.

Rich would shout out, "It's Game Time. My brother has a question to ask."

Tim would stand on a toilet seat and shout out something like, "If you multiply forty-six by twelve and then divide that answer by four, what would you end up with?"

The group toiling away would drop their work tools and don their mental caps but almost always would fail to come up with the correct answer. Failure reached even those who started bringing paper and pencil to get an edge in this battle.

In contrast, Tim's answers to their arithmetic questions were almost always correct. So the genius of the bathroom squad would continue his reign while puzzlement of how x times y would most times elude the actors. Each mistake drew wild laughter.

It pleased Tim that he was so much better at numbers than anyone else. He was the happiest when he could stump Rich who he thought was the smartest and nicest person in the world.

Each member of the company joyfully accepted the fact that they were merely assistants in the company-wide campaign to beautify the house toilets and to keep a smile on Tim's face.

Most of the stellar actors and actresses found great joy that went on in the madness that spilled through what they called the cleaning of their 'frat rooms.'

Their daily leader, Tim, would repeatedly announce and confuse what everyone's assignment was.

All the females acclaimed Tim as the handsomest man in the room but they did little of the work other than going out of their way in muddling their specific assignment.

As they shuttered the doors, Val would turn to Tim, and in as loud a voice as possible, proclaim him to be her favorite boyfriend.

Not that he knew it or cared, Timothy's entire life had been filled with one failure after another. Knowing that he and Rich were the official toilet janitors gave him a sense of self-value that he had never before enjoyed.

Having people call out to him meant he had friends. People showed they valued his friendship and that they liked him. For a person who never before could call anyone his friend, he could now warm to and cherish each hello he got. And, having Val as his girlfriend, led him to being the happiest male in all of Ashland.

Being happy was the most important medicine Tim took.

Chapter Twenty-Seven

Valerie and Rich had become close when they were both cast in the same play. It was really a silly little comedy entitled "The Two of Us" whose humor made it worthy of seeing.

Their small roles in it paid off in a heated love scene that came at the denouement of the play. A kiss that was long in coming ended the scene. Their groping each other was played for laughs and never failed to break up the audience.

The scenes length began to grow as they, two twenty-year olds, confessed a profound distaste for one another. The humor of the scene came from both of their parents who gleefully watched their children begin to discover their counterpart and a slow but burning love affair began to emerge.

Off stage, Valerie seemed more drawn to Tim than Rich who in turn never made one move that showed his liking or disliking Valerie.

It was their fourth week in the run and they were about to finish their last cleaning chore when Valerie approached Rich.

"Hey Rich are you busy now."

"Well, I have to drop off Tim at the house and then I'm free."

"Hey, Tim, can I go along with you and Rich?"

"Sure but Rich always first buys me a chocolate ice cream cone too?"

"I'll get you the double cone if I can get the first and last bite."

With that she grabbed Tim's hand and rushed him out of the room, thus forcing Rich to stumble out after them. The ice cream was purchased with all three sharing the cone, as Tim kept complaining that they were taking bites that were too big.

Fifteen minutes later they dropped Tim off and wordlessly walked off towards Val's apartment. Neither knew which way to walk, but, out of habit, they drifted towards the gravestone that Tim was so taken with. They stopped there for a bit and then started up again. Three or four minutes went by without a word.

Finally Valerie turned to Rich.

"Tell me something when you kiss me in that stupid play of ours what do you feel?"

"I . . . I . . . I don't know. It is the first moment that I realize I love you so I guess I'm happy about that. Yes, I feel happy. What about you?"

"I know that the first time I kissed you I was in pig heaven thinking you really felt something for me. But each kiss became less passionate and now I know that said kiss is just acting for you. You are a good actor, Rich, but I want more from you."

"I'm not sure I know what you are talking about. Please tell me how I am failing you?"

Valerie stopped. She looked at Rich and then pulled him close to her and gave him the most passionate kiss he had ever been given. She finished it off by thrusting her tongue as far down his throat as feasible.

"That's how I feel about you. Why don't you feel that way about me?"

Rich was more than astonished when he realized he had more than enjoyed the experience but equally frightened as he did so. He started to back away from her, but instead he took her hand and walked her to a nearby bench.

He sat her down and then, standing above her took a firm hold on both her shoulders.

"I've got a lot to tell you. I've only told it to one other person and that was a male school teacher friend of mine. So sit here and listen to all I have to say."

With passion he launched into the life he led because of his crazy parents. How they disgusted him with their sexual activities which were done right in front of all the children. He was very young when he first witnessed what he presumed was conventional sex.

"As a result of what I had been exposed to, any thought of my doing any such vile activity disgusted me. For years I went crazy trying to find out what the hell I was. My teacher friend was as straight as can be with a terrific wife and a couple of kids. I learned what a straight family meant. Then Timothy was born, and I could see what real terror he had to face in every part of his life. I fell in love with him because he was so innocent, and I could help him find some joy in life. And all I had to do was to protect him from those monster parents of ours and make certain he knew I was his friend."

"Do you know why I went into theatre? It was because I could lie about who I was and what I wanted out of life. I have never had a boyfriend or a girlfriend. Mostly, I just hated myself for being a nothing."

Tears had started flowing down his cheek, as she pulled him down next to her. Rich buried his head into Valerie's body. He sobbed away as she gently held him in her arms.

"Rich, I think I know you better than you know yourself. I love our on-stage kiss whether it is mere acting or not. I love everything about you."

For the first time in his life Rich took both his hands and clasped a woman's face in them. Slowly he drew Valerie to his lips and he kissed her. This was no stage kiss. It was a man gently telling his woman how much he loved her.

Rich hardly slept that night. He went to bed thinking of Valerie. He turned on the little radio that he kept buried beneath his pillow and thought of Valerie. He awoke at 2:32 a.m. and thought of Valerie

When he awoke again at 4:02 he couldn't fall asleep at all. At 7:00 a.m., his normal wake up time, he started getting dressed. Through the remainder of the morning he thought and thought of nothing but Valerie.

That afternoon "The Two of Us" matinee ended rather oddly as the kissing scene lasted far longer than normally. It got to the point that the actor playing the girl's father, while visibly hiding off stage, shouted out 'Enough already' and then burst into hilarious laughter.

The audience exploded with their laughter.

Backstage the stage manager screamed at his assistant, "I love it. Let's keep it in."

Chapter Twenty-Eight

$\mathcal{R}$ ich realized that the new emotion he felt towards Valerie brought with it constant fear. How could he keep this beautiful creature? She was too bright, too beautiful, too spirited, too vivacious, too, too, too, well just too much for anyone as dull as he was.

Their moments together since the on stage explosion was akin to a constant affair that kept screaming out 'We are the greatest lovers of all time."

He never dared ask her of previous romances she might have had.

She was opposite of him in her willingness to tell him anything about her past. She dared doing both verbal and physical actions that frightened him silly. Where he feared to try anything new, she was ready to shake up the world.

Typical was his reaction to the simple question she posed very early one morning, "I think we should move in together."

To which he screamed "You want to do what?"

"You know, Rich, I don't know why I love you so much. The answer to your question is simple enough. It's basic economics. We move to one apartment that is much more beautiful than each of our current places and it will cost us far less for the one apartment than what we are now shelling out for the two places."

She then pushed him into her bed and smothered him with kisses. Rich responded with yet another question, "But how do we handle Tim?"

"That's the easiest part. He has bedroom number one and we have bedroom number two. When I tire of making love with you, I will start sharing his room, and you bring in some floozy you like more than you like me."

With that she jumped away and screamed for Tim to join them. Within seconds Tim was at their side. He was wearing long johns, a blue striped shirt and boots.

"What's cooking?"

"I've got to ask you a question that means much to me. Okay?"

"Sure. And I'll ask you one."

"No. I just want your answer to my question."

"Okay. Shoot."

Valerie then laid out all the reasons for the three of them to start living together.

Tim offered a puzzled response. "I don't understand. Don't we live together now?"

And with that he turned away and went back to the living room television set which was blaring away with a cooking show. They were making Tamales which were one of his favorite foods.

Valerie turned to Rich flipped her hands out to him and in the quietest of voices asked, "Any further problems?"

Chapter Twenty-Nine

he first person to be told about Valerie and Rich of
course had to be Tony. That night after tucking Tim
into bed they headed off for his cabin which was at the top
of Mountain Cemetery.

It was almost midnight when they burst in on their friend.

Tony was not the best of sleepers and therefore greeted
them with a seriously dour face. "What in the hell are you
two lunatics doing here?"

Rich jumped atop Tony and advised Valerie that he
had this idiot under control and to go ahead and tell him
her story.

With sincere passion the words came out from her about
what had started as a silly boyfriend-girlfriend affair that
had now grown into a newly discovered love affair.

Val added that what was a silly little affair had blossomed
into her loving him and wanting to marry him.

Tony managed to slip away from Rich before shouting
out at them in a very strong tone. "Are you both crazy?"

They were stunned by his response. Even Rich was angered.

"Wait one minute you two. There isn't a chance in hell that Tim could handle a love affair. How could you believe Tim is ready for some hot love affair?"

"What the hell are you talking about?" immediately came forth from both Val and Rich.

"I mean Tim is hardly ready for some crazed love affair, and I cannot see how you two could think I'm wrong. Rich, have you agreed to this crazy match? You want to do this?"

Rich offered a simple answer "I don't understand. What match are you talking about?"

"Valerie, how many times have I heard you declare that Tim was your boyfriend? And now it has grown into a very mushy love affair. You are both out of your minds."

Valerie was the first to get it and burst into laughter. Not a moment later Rich fell to the floor convulsed with wild guffaws. Their hysteria kept increasing.

Tony, sporting as huge a frown as he ever had, kept asking what was so funny.

Rich managed to hysterically squeeze out that Tony had somehow come to a conclusion that was about the nuttiest thing he had ever head and that he was certain Val thought so as well.

She was so engulfed with laughter that she could not utter one sensible word.

Some five minutes later Valerie managed to gain control of her laughter and very softly managed to get out one serious sentence.

"Tony, let me make a confession. Yes, I am in love with Tim but I am certain it is the same love that you and Rich have for Tim."

At that point both Rich and Val went hysterical with laughter. It took many moments before Rich could speak words that made some sense.

"Tony, I hate to change your very strange thoughts but Val telling all about her and Tim being lovers was never more than a laugh she used to keep Tim happy. Her boy-friend and real love is named Rich not Tim."

Valerie added that she had tried to make it with Tim but that he had turned her down flat cold.

"So I had to settle for Rich. If he wouldn't go along with me I was going to hit on you."

"And I would have turned you down flat. Nobody likes pushy broads like you."

Tony plaintively asked Valerie, "Does Tim know that he is not your boyfriend anymore?"

Those words brought forth another laughter outburst from all present. Rich summed up the entire discussion by telling Tony that he had told Tim that he could be Valerie's number one boy-friend whenever he wanted to.

Later that day Tim strolled into Tony's office. He didn't offer a word but just sat in the corner chair with a puzzled look on his face. Tony knew something was bothering Tim but offered nothing to break the silence.

Finally, Tim opened up by asking Tony if he could ask him a rough question that he could only talk about with him.

Tony spit three times and offered, "You have my word that I'll never breathe a word of anything you tell me."

Tim nodded and quickly said "I think my brother and Valerie are in love with each other and I'm not sure if they want me around.

"Tim don't be such a goofus. They both love you more than they love each other and that love makes the world a better place."

"Okay then I love you too, and what does goofus mean?"

Chapter Thirty

Valerie awakened quite early that morning with thoughts of a new adventure for Richard and herself. She immediately started tugging at the still fast asleep Rich.

After much shouting and tugging, Rich opened his eyes. Dazedly he stared at her.

"Hey Babe, what's up?"

"Rich we are going to celebrate. Do you hear me? We must honor this great pact we have made."

"Could you give me another try at that?"

Valerie kept her patience as she very slowly repeated. "We are going to honor this relationship we have fashioned."

"No, I had nothing to do with that great whatever you have come up with. It was all you."

"That doesn't matter. What is of concern is that we will be free of the Oregon Shakespeare Festival for almost three full days after Sunday's matinee. We are out of this town from late Sunday afternoon till Wednesday afternoon."

By now she was hurriedly donning her clothes and rushing to the bathroom. There was much to set in motion. She left a totally confused Rich certain that once he heard the complete plan he still wouldn't understand what she was talking about.

She next dashed into Tim's room, planted a big kiss on his still asleep face and then bolted out the front door. Two hours later she charged back into the apartment with a raft of maps and brochures.

Rich awaited the onslaught but, oddly enough, she ignored him completely and walked directly into Tim's room.

"Hi Val, what's cooking?"

"Tell me something, Tim. Have you ever heard of Mt. Ashland?"

It took him some time to go through the thinking process but finally he told her that Tony had spoken of it lots of times.

"He said it is the highest mountain around here and some day he is going to take me camping up at its peak."

She handed him half of the sheets she had carried and dashed into the kitchen where Rich was preparing breakfast for the three of them.

"Where did you fly to?"

"Read this. It's where we are going to this coming Sunday."

"Where we are doing what?"

"How long have we been together?"

"That's one I can answer. I've been in heaven for almost one solid month."

With that, he dove at her. It was a perfect tackle. She screamed, "Sir, please be kind to me. I am a virgin so spare me from any coarse activity."

"You are a what? Ha. What you are is the biggest liar to ever live in Ashland."

"Call me what you want. I shall confess my sins in church.

He sniffed at her neck as he asked, "Okay. Let's have it all."

"That's easy. No show Sunday night and we are off until Wednesday evening. So we can be in San Francisco by early Sunday evening. We check into some posh hotel for three nights. The first night we have a late dinner at some spiffy restaurant. Monday, Tuesday and Wednesday we are free to do whatever we want. Late Wednesday we leave for home and our careers as the world's greatest young actors."

She then went on detailing all they would see and do in the time they spent in San Francisco.

"We will scour all of Frisco's wonderful sights and take in some theatre. Which I am certain we will hate. But, each night we will have the greatest sex that has ever been performed by two such as us."

Rich stared at her for less than a moment and then exclaimed, "I'm glad you came up with all of that but do we just shoot Tim or let him wander the streets while we are enjoying Frisco."

"You are a simpleton. Tim and Tony will be camping out on Mt. Ashland while we are in Frisco. They haven't agreed to that as yet but they will tonight when we advise them of what they will be doing."

It did not take any effort to convince Tony and Tim of what they would be doing while they were in San Francisco. Of course, Tim went out of his mind with the thought of climbing up Mt. Ashland

The Tony response was exactly as expected.

"You mean Tim and I will be rid of you two pains in the ass for three days? You want us to be up on top of Ashland doing whatever we want to. It will be difficult for us to do same but to enable you two to enjoy yourself I think we can handle that chore."

Chapter Thirty-One

*I*t seemingly took weeks for Sunday afternoon to finally arrive. Valerie, Tim and Rich were anxiously awaiting the arrival of Tony. Within seconds they heard him shouting from the street below.

"Hey you lazy bums are you ever going to get your asses down here?"

In an earlier meeting Tony had told Tim that Mt. Ashland was a full four thousand and thirty three feet high which meant nothing to Tim other than that sounded very tall which totally excited him.

Tony had also discussed the glories of camping atop Mt. Ashland. Some years back he had done a solo climb up the mountain and he knew that Tim would love it as much as he did.

That just the two of them would be on top of a spectacular mountain that rated as one of the highest peaks in Southern Oregon had Tim atremble.

Other than a swift kiss from Valerie to Tim and Tony the two couples swiftly parted.

Rich and Valerie were soon at the Medford Airport awaiting their planes departure, while Tim and Tony were swiftly spinning their way up to the mountain top of Mt. Ashland. They took to singing made up verses about Tony's old car which made their climb up the hill so easy.

The mountain climbing group had hardly gone half way up Mt. Ashland before they made their first camp-fire, cooked four hot dogs which they quickly devoured and were asleep as close to the fire as they could get.

It took but a few hours before Valerie and Rich were standing at the front desk of a modest looking hotel called the Mossel Inn. They had debated quite seriously about luxuriating at some posh hotel which they figured meant spending at least $200.00 per night or more, but they opted to save a few bucks by staying at a more mod-est site.

They were rather shocked to hear an officious voice peal out from behind the front desk that the Mossel Inn's lowest room price was $325.00.

Rich made the decision quite easily. He walked over to a young lad wearing a bellboy's uniform. Rich pulled a five dollar bill from his pocket and handed it to the boy before saying a word. A brief conversation was then held between the two.

 Rich turned back to Valerie and picked up the two little bags they had as he turned towards the front door. In a fraudulent English accent he called out "Do come along darling we are due to spend our nights elsewhere."

And, just round the corner, they found the lovely "Come on Inn" Bed and Breakfast. It was as lovely a place as they could have hoped for. The reception they received was as gracious as could be. The room proved to be perfect with a cost per night that was far less than half the price offered at the Mossel and included a sumptuous breakfast.

The theatre they attended that first night was very special. It gave them the feeling that they were in one of the New York's grand theatres. Unfortunately, the show they viewed left them totally disappointed.

Snobbishly, they agreed that it surely wasn't even close to the work they all did in Ashland.

Ever full of ideas, Valerie popped up with her most outrageous thought. As they left the theatre she excitedly turned to Rich.

"That dreadful show had a packed house. I hated the performance but it gave me a great idea. Why don't we move down here and open our own theatre. The work we turn out will be far better than what we just witnessed, and we will make a fortune because of the quality of our productions."

"Wow, what a great idea. I bet I have at least five hundred bucks in savings and you probably have the same amount. So we come down here and stage the epic play I have written. Its title is "The Beggars of San Francisco."

Those words would normally have prompted anything in Valerie's hand being thrown swiftly at Rich's face. Fortunately, she was empty handed so that Rich escaped unharmed other than Val screaming at him that she definitively hated everything about the man she loved.

She sneered at him and snapped out. "I don't see why I care for you. You never dream. I'm moving into Tim's bed. He's always fun and welcoming."

Rich's cruel reply about her ability to handle Tim's tendency to wet the bed quickly cut Valerie short. She rarely brought up that idea again, but she kept dreaming of opening their very own theatre which would be a mighty success from the very first.

.

Chapter Thirty-Two

The next morning they rose extremely early, stuffed themselves silly on the best breakfast they had ever eaten and then tore out to begin their trip through the city. Valerie had mapped out a series of daytime visits which included stops at places like Alcatraz, the Golden Gate Bridge, Chinatown, the Cable Car System, as well as the unique Fisherman's Wharf and the attendant seals that whirled throughout the surrounding waters.

The seals seemed to endlessly swim up and down the waters merely to catch their eyes. Valerie picked out two which she compared to Caruso and Callas for the honking they kept sending out for all the tourists to enjoy.

Rich, ever the kill joy, laughingly dared her to explain how she got to comparing these sweet seals to those operatic egotists. To which she accused him of having no imagination.

"It is obvious to me that their egos are very comparable to those of Caruso and Callas. Without a question their antics are just to catch our eyes and applause."

This brought on a good deal of prolonged discussion about whether Caruso or Callas were more dramatic than seals.

Rich quietly suffered much of Valerie's arguing for the smaller of the two Seals before he countered by saying,

"And you are comparable to both of those egotistical nut cases."

She simply laughed off Rich's barb by sharply proclaiming that she had never understood why she fell in love with a man who has not had a pleasant thought since his last turn at masturbation.

With that comment, Valerie's entered a rather spiffy shop. Her fellow customers and the owner of the shop turned their ears to the very pretty yet foul mouthed young woman. However, to Valerie, they were not eavesdroppers. They were a very attentive audience who were glued to her performance.

Valerie and Rich did better than most in resisting the ever constant sales pitches thrown at them but by later that day, their freshly counted items were as plentiful as any of their fellow travelers.

What had equally captivated our youthful voyagers were the sleek boats that steamed up and down the nearby waters. They came in all sizes and shapes yet carried with them a unique joie-de-vive that delighted all of the on board passengers as well as those who ogled them from the shore.

The slickness of the boats forced Valerie and Rich to purchase tickets for a trip around the harbor and an adventure they would never forget.

The two were rushing towards the boat's gangplank which they were about to get on when Valerie inadvertently bumped into a man who was blocking the first steps up.

Actually bumped is a gross overstatement. Brushed would be a more accurate description statement of what had occurred. She never could see how he could go sprawling on such a gentle tap. In falling he toppled the ice cream cone he was chomping on. The ice cream fell across his face. He instantly started screaming as if he had been hit by an axe.

To Valerie and Rich, the man had been barely touched. How he had gotten into the violent screams he was now directing at Val was beyond them. The man was unshaven and dressed rather sloppily. The odor that he was sporting seemed to be pouring from him. Sweat was flowing down his face which made him also look all the grosser. The small ice cream cone hitting his face set off a series of vile words about how badly he was injured. There wasn't a clean word used in his entire expletive.

Valerie, the sweetest of all people, tried apologizing to the man but all to no avail. Hoping to stop the flow of curse words she turned and tore off to a small ice cream shop at the foot of the street where she purchased the largest cone available.

Racing back she saw the Captain of the ship pick up the man she thought she had injured and smacked him across the head.

"Listen, you little bastard, how many times have I told you to stay away from my ship with that baloney injury nonsense?"

With that he delivered a hefty boot to the man's backside which sent him flying. He intensified his screams once he got away from the gangplank. All of his venom was directed towards Valerie.

It did not deter her from offering the ice cream cone to the man. He snatched it from Valerie and then promptly flung it back at her face which instantly became covered with the lush ice cream mixture.

His expletives were filled with the coarsest of filth. The foulest words to come from his mouth were spit forth directly on Valerie.

"You hurt me you miserable little shit, and I'm not going to let you get away with it. Never, never you rich bitch."

With that he spun away from them and rapidly limped off. Every few feet he would stop and turn back to Valerie so that he could spit out more expletives back at her.

As he turned the corner from the boat he dug his hands into his pant's pocket and pulled out Valerie's purse. Snitching it had been as easy as pie. Everybody was so confused what with all the noise he was making he was the only one who knew what was going on. In fact he thought he should thank the Captain for the kick in the pants which allowed him to get away from all of them.

When he was a block away he opened Valerie's purse and found he had scored big time. First off there was over $315 in cash. He knew he couldn't use the Visa or American Express cards but he did know who to sell them to. It was a real killing for him.

Searching through her bag gave him all sorts of information about her. Obviously, she must be some rich bitch who lived in Ashland, Oregon. He had heard of Ashland and the tons of rich people who lived there. It dawned on him that he should pay her a visit in Ashland and go after another big score.

Oddly enough there was one thing about her that bothered him. Her face seemed familiar to him.

Going through the remainder of her purse he came across a solo shot of the girl. He murmured out loud that she sure was a pretty one and that she sure does look something like Melissa, but she isn't half as pretty as his cousin, Melissa.

The Melissa /Valerie resemblance stirred thoughts of how as a kid he had lived within one block of Melissa. They were cousins and he made her home his second home. A dire recollection reopened his distaste for Melissa and the way she would always laugh at him when he tried getting close to her. A second thought flashed at him with much pain as he envisioned his father beating him for his cursing out at Melissa.

It infuriated Irvine, a name which he had always hated, that the one pleasure he got at home was beating up his little brother or stealing money out of his mother's pocket book.

Outside the house he got great joy from breaking store windows or swiping things from same enterprises. He didn't have one kid that he could call a friend. He would beat up the small kids and stay away from the big guys on the block. His greatest pleasure was doing one thing or another that would piss off others and then racing off before they could catch him and beat the hell out of him.

What particularly bothered Valerie about the entire incident was that the dreadful man who had rough-necked her seemed to know who she was. The more the day passed without her determining who he was the more she was certain that somehow she knew him.

Chapter Thirty-Three

$\mathcal{V}$alerie kept recalling the ship's Captain laughing as he assured Valerie not to worry.

"He is just a street bum, and you'll never see him again. He'll probably turn up here soon enough and start another scrap with one of my passengers. The next time that happens I'll get him thrown into the hoosegow."

Richard thanked the Captain then threw his arms around the still weeping Valerie. He next hailed a cab and they set off for their lovely bed and breakfast. It was but twenty minutes later when Valerie collapsed onto her bed.

Slowly she began to regain her self-control.

"Rich could you please get me my purse?"

"Sure thing where is it?"

"I'm not certain. I may have dropped it in the bathroom."

Rich thoroughly searched the entire suite but still could not find the purse. He even looked under the bed and then searched through the items they had purchased that morning but all was for naught.

He asked Valerie if she could recall when she last had it. The best she could think of was buying the ice cream cone and feeling loaded down with it and her purse.

He raced down to the reception area hoping to find it there but found nothing. In turning towards the street, he glanced outside and, wonder of wonders, saw the same cab driver that they had just used to get to the hotel. The driver was standing outside his cab patiently awaiting his next fare to appear.

Rich rushed out to the cab and quickly offered a brief explanation of his dilemma. He and the driver scoured the cab thoroughly only to find no bag anywhere. Within minutes they sped back to the boat they had seemingly just left.

It was a fruitless search of the boat and quickly Rich returned to their room empty handed.

"Rich, can I ask a favor of you? Can we pack up and go home. I feel terrible and I want to be home with you and Tim and Tony.

Within four hours they were in the sky and within three additional hours she was lying in her own bed. She was sad and still frightened but no tears graced her face.

Chapter Thirty-Four

$\mathcal{V}$alerie and Rich arrived home a full two days before Tim and Tony. The hikers were enjoying their adventures in every moment atop the mountain. Even on the trip down the mountain he found joy thinking of all the marvelous moments he and Tony had on top of the mountain. The most exciting time for Tim was that in the almost four days on the peak they had run into all sorts of animals but never did they see another human being.

Reporting back to his brother, Tim raved about trying to talk to the rabbits and the little skunks which would sit a few feet away from them and just stare at these new beings that had moved into their homeland.

Tony said it was just like the time when the Indians were invaded by the gold seekers so many years ago. The only difference was that the invaders, Tony and Tim, were not attacked by the birds or animals of the mountains for doing any harm to the beautiful mountain top. The less interest the invaders showed in them the closer the original group came to them. But neither side showed much interest in the other and that seemed to please all.

Rich and Valerie offered no tales other than they had loved San Francisco and would certainly get back there someday. They did not relate one word about their awful event on the wharf.

On the other hand, Tony and Tim could not stop raving about the wonders of nature. There was little doubt about which group had a better time.

Valerie had, of course, canceled her credit cards and obtained new ones. She also refilled her new purse with all the pertinent information she needed. It seemed like a perfect bore to continue to stuff paper after paper back into her purse even though she rarely used any of the information that was filling up her bag.

One habit underwent a massive change. She never again was casual in her handling of her purse. It was either clutched tightly in her left hand or tightly held in her right hand coat pocket.

Not once did she talk about the awful experience in San Francisco to any of her friends and that included Tony. Rich, however, spent much time telling Tony about Valerie's frightening adventure.

"What puzzles me most is the way Val reacted to that dreadful man who caused all the problems. The Captain said he was just a bum off the streets and that assurance should have blown the entire incident away. But no, she had to rush off to fetch the bum an ice cream cone to make that bum feel better. How she lost her purse was beyond me. We were having the time of our lives and suddenly this strongest of strong women just fell apart. What really beats me is that she keeps talking about the bum who assaulted her and that he looked familiar to her."

"Rich, it sure beats me. Do you think she knew him or he reminded her of somebody she knew?" That thought lingered with Rich for some time. Many times he was tempted to ask her about same, but he avoided going down that dangerous path.

They were back on schedule working hard and enjoying every moment of it, but Valerie was not her usual fun self. She had extended periods of depression with no apparent rationale for what caused her changes in mood.

Chapter Thirty-Five

im had gone to bed. Rich and Valerie were as usual catching the last moments of the Stephen Colbert TV Show. Colbert was extolling the value of probing questions being used to maintain a relationship.

Those comments prompted Rich to turn and ask Val if he could get the answer to something that was bothering him. "It's a question that's probably the stupidest question I could ask you."

"Well, if it is that stupid I'll probably give you a stupid answer right back."

Rich rose from his soft chair picked up the remote and shut off the TV.

"Hey, what goes on? I was enjoying that bit."

Rich crossed over to where she was sitting and gently plucked her up and into his arms. He was embracing her very tightly when he asked if she knew how much he loved her.

"Oh, I know you don't love me, but you like using me for varied sexual purposes."

"Right on. And here is the question of the evening. It requires our going back to that awful afternoon in Frisco. I've been bothered many times with the craziest of ideas from which comes this question. Did that Bum remind you of someone?"

She jumped out of his arms and kneeled facing him.

"Do I talk in my sleep? Have we ever discussed this before? Why do you ask that question?"

"Because I haven't stopped wondering about what could shake someone as strong as you are into such a pathetic figure. You come out of it, but every now and then, I see vestiges of the woman I love, and I can't understand what drives her to this lesser self."

"Wow. This is outstanding. Every moment since Frisco I have had that question and no, I don't have an answer, except that from the first moment I looked into his face, I thought I knew him."

"And did anything come of that?"

"Not really, but I recalled one night back home when I was quite young, and I asked Grandma why she was crying. I can't recall her answer but her words seem to say something like why did he do such a terrible thing?"

She also recalled a picture that elicited a big spat between her father and mother. She sensed her father grabbing the photo from her mother and tearing it into pieces and tossing it into the fireplace. The man in the picture had the same blondish looking hair that seemed to resemble Mom's hair.

It took but seconds and she was on the phone talking to her mother. In their conversation, Valerie did query her about a strange memory she had about her mother and father arguing about an old picture. She got no worthwhile response.

"Oh, just forget it and get out here as soon as you can. I've got someone to introduce you to"

"Does that mean that you've finally met a man?"

"Get out here, and I might answer that query."

Chapter Thirty-Six

The past three weeks had not been much fun for Irvine. He had tried to play the gangplank bit again, but the ship's Captain had caught him and beat the living hell out of him. Another Captain had gotten the cops to haul him in for loitering and that got him a week in the toughest jail in town.

Almost as soon as he entered the cell, he tried to gain stature with some of his fellow cell mates by giving them some loud mouthed shit. They rewarded him with a far worse beating than the Captain had delivered. Thereafter, he kept his lips tightly shut for the rest of his jail stay.

For causing the uprising in the cell and the serious injury he had given to one of the oldest inmates, he got an additional three months behind bars.

Each day of those months heightened his bitterness at the world and everything it stood for. This was no new found emotion for Irvine. His hatred for humanity had been with him since his earliest days. Even then there was little love coming back from his parents who had little faith in their ne'er-do-well offspring.

It was early evening when Irvine was finally released from the horrid jail he was confined to. He hurried off to the little room he called home. He was looking forward to a quiet night's sleep in the soft bed that he so loved.

As he neared his flat he happily recalled how he had found the place. He had been strolling through a rather down-trodden neighborhood when he saw some scruffy looking guys fill up their car with clothes and some furniture. As they sped off, the door to their flat was left wide open. The moment the car disappeared from sight, he peered into the dingy room. To his delight he saw a single bed, a small table and two chairs. It smelled like home to Irvine. Obviously no one owned this dire room, but to Irvine he had found his new residence.

He rushed off to a nearby junk yard where he found a beaten up toilet. It had taken him much time to find what he thought would be the perfect toilet. Yet he wondered if it would fit into his horrid little room. He tried to get some kind of lock for the front door but he knew he would first have to repair the entrance to his new shelter. Nevertheless, he was delighted with his new found home.

Fresh from that far from comfortable jailing he was all smiles as he threw open the door to his flat. As he entered back into his little, but loved room he found two rather pathetic women seated in his apartment.

They looked up as Irvine entered the room and told him he had come into the wrong place.

"This ain't no wrong place? Listen, you two ugly pieces of shit, I'm going to give you ten minutes to get the hell out of my place. So start moving before I get angry and beat the living hell out of you."

The one who had spoken nicely to him rose from her chair. She slowly walked to where he was standing. When she came face to face with Irvine, she immediately smashed his face with a solid right fist. As he started falling she kicked him several times right in the testicles. She then picked up his limp body and dragged it out to the street and tossed it into the gutter. She gave him one more solid kick and spit directly into his face. He didn't even see her calmly turn back into the apartment.

He lay there wondering what in the hell the world had against him and decided it was everyone in San Francisco that hated him.

He got to thinking of the last killing he had made. This brought back thoughts of that rich Ashland bitch. He dragged himself up and as he did so, he espied a beaten car that sat outside a bakery while the driver was delivering the breads for the day. It soon was his.

Sure enough the car was idling away with the key in its start position, which allowed him to jump behind the steering wheel and speed off. God had gifted him with the biggest score of his life. He knew that he must get out of Frisco as soon as possible.

He drove off northwards knowing that he was going to get even with the entire world that he so hated. He would start with the little bitch from the dock. That little Ashland whore would pay again for what he had endured these past months. Soon he would be rolling in cash.

His need for hard cash was solved when he garnered a valuable amount of cash from selling the fresh breads from the car. This allowed him to fill up the gas tank and take off for Ashland, Oregon. He kept thinking about that little town that soon was to be his haven.

As he crossed the San Francisco Bridge, he started singing his favorite song. It was a Merle Haggard piece that everyone in his original family would sing in the good old days. He had grown up singing that song. Those were the days he most missed. A time when he could do whatever he wanted to do.

His spitting in the face of his entire family finally resulted with his very own mother tossing him out of the house. He hated each and every one of his family. No one ever understood him. Somehow, someway, he would get even with those bastards.

He felt positive that Ashland was the first step forward in bringing him to the happiness he deserved.

He felt elated and started singing out.

"Think about a Lullaby, Baby
Close your eyes. Don't cry
Think about a Lullaby
Let me sing you off to sleep
Let me pray your soul to keep
It's safe here with your Mom and I
Think about a butterfly
Think about a lullaby
Think about a lullaby
Think about a cloud in the sky
You can count your little sheep
But Babe, Please don't cry

He sang the song again and again then suddenly stopped. Rather fiercely he rolled down the driver's window and shouted out as loud and as angrily as he could to the entire world. "I will show them. I will show them all."

Chapter Thirty-Seven

*J*t was late evening as he slowly drove the heap to a quiet Ashland side street. He carefully parked it under a tree with massive branches hanging down over the car and headed off to the theatre. All the information that he had taken from her bag had assured him she was an actress in the big theatre in town.

It took him almost fifteen minutes of searching poster after poster all of which publicized what would be done that evening. It was the sheet telling of the show being done at the Bowmer Theatre that her face jumped off with the information he needed.

An enormous smile came across his face. He knew that winning days were coming his way.

He took the time to buy a rather large hat that more than covered his face. He asked a person who seemed to know what was going on where the actors came out of the theatre after the show was over and was very politely told to sit on the bricks that faced a specific door.

"It may be as much as an hour or so before that show is over but I promise it won't be much longer than that when the actors will start pouring out of that door

He thanked the young lady who had been so helpful. Then he lost himself in the crowds, who were obviously on the same wait as he was.

It was exactly fifty minutes before he spied Valerie amidst half a dozen other people emerge from said door. It seemed like all were gabbing away at the same time but, bit by bit, the crowd dispersed in many directions. He kept his eyes on his target and the young man she clung to. He quickly determined that the man she was arm in arm with was that same fellow he said seen in Frisco.

It was a beautifully calm and clear night both in the climate and the joy Irvine was experiencing.

The pace his couple took was rather leisurely and his eyes never left his target. The walk stretched into some twenty minutes before they paused at a modest house. She handed the man a batch of packages and garments but held onto her purse.

She started walking off as her very handsome man dashed into the house. He turned at the door and then turned back as she shouted out to him, "I want you to know that you are the favorite man I am sleeping with these days."

He turned completely to her and casually shouted back, "Sure, all the other guys are gay and they don't have a clue as how one satisfies a wanton woman like you. Say Hi to Tony for me, and tell him I'll see him tomorrow morning and tell Tim to move his ass as you bring him down from Tony's."

They threw each other kisses as he turned into the building and she started joyfully into the treed area across the street.

Her pace was rather slow as there was no pressure to get to Tony's rather rustic abode. She had no sense of anyone following her and was looking forward to picking up Tim and the oncoming pleasure she would have gossiping with Tony.

Tony anticipated with much joy her coming and the little chat they would have before she took Tim back home. It was a bit dark to allow Tim to saunter home alone from Tony's cabin.

Equally, Valerie knew both Tim and Tony would greet her with great joy. Bit by bit she climbed deeper and deeper into the woods. The dirt path she was on was as dead quiet as could be but it didn't bother her at all.

Irvine on the other hand was as tense as could be. He didn't have a clue as to where she was going, nor where the hell her hoity-toity boyfriend had gone off to. He kept on her left waiting for the proper spot to grab her.

Joyfully, he could see that she held her purse tightly with her right hand. Both hands were swinging away in tempo with her feet.

Irvine slowly started creeping up to her. Not too far ahead he spotted a small cabin and decided to make his move now so as to avoid any people popping up from that little cabin. They were but a few feet from the darkened cabin as he picked up his pace, and within seconds he was right behind her.

Without saying a word, he took the heavy stick he had been carrying and swung it. He had meant to hit her in the head but she bent her head at that very moment and the impact landed on her back.

"Well, you sweet little cunt, we meet again and this time I intend to beat the living hell out of you. When I'm through with you you'll never forget who you dared mess with."

She let out a mighty scream as she fell and rolled sideways. As she did so, she managed to get a short glance at the face of this crazy man who was attacking her. She was further terrified when that glance seemed to shout out to her 'It's the man from San Francisco.'

Not a word came forth from her, but inwardly words seemed to scream out, 'It is him – that crazed man from Frisco.'

She sank deeply into the sandy ground. He had not killed her but he had definitely rendered her unconscious. The bag she carried assured him that he soon would be back in the chips.

His preoccupation with her goods prevented him from hearing the stealthy sounds of a man creeping up on him. It was Tony who but moments before had been conversing with Tim, who had fallen fast asleep as they talked.

The unusual clamor outside the little cabin drew Tony out into the black night. It took but seconds for Tony to scream out, "Drop that stick and get away from that girl."

Irvine reacted as he had taught himself. When you are in danger whip out your forty five and fire away. Two bullets flew towards Tony. Neither missed their mark, and Tony fell dead before he hit the floor.

Irvine, purse in hand, was gone in but a few seconds.

Rich was wasting some time with putting away the packages they had bought earlier. He took a last look around the apartment and finding all was well he just threw on an old jacket and rushed out to the path that he knew Valerie had taken.

Thinking she and Tony might be talking, he raced towards the cabin. It took but ten minutes for Rich to espy what looked like two bodies sprawled out in the dirt in front of the cabin. As he sped forward he spied Valerie lying face down just off the path.

Horrific screams poured from his mouth.

Neither body moved so much as an inch. He dropped to his knees beside Valerie, as she slowly moved her head. Almost immediately a low moan came forth assuring him that she was on the verge of awakening. His voice grew stronger as he held his love and pleaded with her to awaken.

Slowly her eyes opened wilder and she seemed to recognize who was holding her. His joy increased with every word she spoke.

It was just seconds later that she raised one finger and pointed it at the body lying above her. Only one word accompanied her gesture, "TONY."

Rich spun over to the male body and saw the blood pouring out of his chest

Valerie tried rising, but all she could do was to prop herself up on one elbow as she feebly asked two tear-filled questions. "Was I right? Is it Tony?"

"Later honey, we'll talk about Tony later."

He gently pulled Valerie over to the nearest tree and eased her against it. He saw that she had been badly frightened but seemed to be fine other than that. He threw his jacket around her and then spun back to the other body.

This body did not move nor did it seem to be breathing. Within seconds of holding the body Rich knew that his dearest friend was dead. Slowly he managed to get the body face up. Rich's eyes were engulfed with tears as he ever so slowly wiped all the blood and dirt from the body of his very best friend. He gently hugged Tony's body. All he could say was one word which he repeated and repeated.

"No, no, no."

Tony, the wonderful, full of life man, lay dead in Rich's arms.

He awkwardly covered the dead body with his jacket, as he realized that they would never again laugh with this man who was superior to all other men, nor would Tony ever again educate these so devoted friends of his.

He carried his quiet tears back with him to Valerie in an attempt to wordlessly comfort her. He spun her head away from Tony. He could do nothing to quell the tears that totally engulfed her. Within seconds the two clutched each other in endless moans and tears.

The resultant cacophony drew everyone on the nearby streets racing towards them. Shortly afterwards a policeman joined the crowd. He took one look and instantly called out, "My god, "It's going to be 1858 all over again."

Chapter Thirty-Eight

That night there was no sleep for Valerie or Rich. It seemed as if every police officer in the station house wanted to just talk to them, to see them, or to interview them. The fact of the matter was that only the Chief of Police and the head Detective were given that opportunity.

By the next day everybody in Ashland knew of what had transpired the previous evening. The Festival instantly gave Valerie as much time off as she felt she needed. Rich, as a buttress to her battles joined her for the first week; however, he quickly found that it was better for him to get the release he needed by going back on stage.

Less than twenty-four hours later, Melissa Crawford, Valerie's mother, arrived in Ashland. It was the perfect medicine for Valerie and Rich, both of whom quickly found that Mother Crawford possessed the words and the sensitivity to face each day easing the pain that coursed through her beloved daughter. Rich helped but it was Mom who woke her from the darkness she lived in.

Time after time Valerie screamed out that she was the cause of Tony's death.

Her mother always replied, "Did you see the killer? Could you identify the killer? What makes you so clairvoyant?"

Valerie's response would always bring them back to San Francisco.

"Everything bad that has happened since we were in Frisco was caused by me. It is always me. I forced Rich to go there. "

"Well Miss Trouble Maker did you recognize the man who attacked you here. Oh, I remember. You never saw him, so you really can't in any way identify him."

Slowly reality found its place in Valerie's heart but deep down in her soul she firmly believed that somehow she was the cause of both of those terrors that had invaded her life.

Mom was an ongoing blessing. A hug from Mom lessened the torrent of tears from Val. A kiss from Mom eased the pains that tore her face apart. Mom's ever constant words was full of love and peace and gently steered Val to thoughts of peace and beauty.

What most plagued her were the horrible thoughts that kept going through her brain. Above all she couldn't stop thinking that she had caused the death of her wonderful friend.

It took several days before she realized that once again her purse was gone. The thoughts awakened pains in her heart. The purse meant nothing but the other pains merely grew worse.

Though she had no tangible proof of it, she kept saying that the man who had attacked her and killed Tony was the maniac who had assaulted her in San Francisco.

Those words propelled Melissa Crawford into action. The more she heard Val talk of her attacker, the more she geared up to go into partnership with the local police department.

One afternoon, while Valerie was taking a nap, she sauntered down to the Police headquarters and asked to see the Chief of Police. The request was not greeted with a welcoming ear. The officer seated at the front desk was willing to take down the information she had, and in that way get her message through to the Chief.

Melissa tried to cover her disdain for the young man and gently said he must have misunderstood her request. She repeated that she had to see the Chief, but the officer started to cut her off.

"My good friend, I am attempting to give your Chief information about the murder that occurred just a few days ago in this hick town, but you seem determined to prevent that from happening."

He hadn't gotten through four words in response before Melissa broke through with, "Listen you little pissant, I'm not here to play word games with you."

Those words were delivered at a rather loud volume. She continued with, "Now get that Chief of yours out here right now, or I am going to call my husband who is the Chief of a police department that makes this place look like an ant hill and have him give your chief a real good chewing out."

This brief berating brought out a very angry Chief of Police.

She took a far more affable tone with the Chief. First she thanked him for giving her a few moments of his very busy day.

"But I wouldn't bother you if I didn't think I had pertinent information about that horrid murder last week. First, you should know that it was my daughter who was beaten by the killer and, secondly, I believe I know who the killer is."

With that the Chief asked her to come into his office, offered her a cup of coffee, which she thanked him for but turned down.

Instead she proffered one short sentence.

"I believe the killer is my cousin!"

Of all the statements that the Chief thought might be uttered, those were the least expected. She, however, did not allow him to say a word or pose a question.

"I have a cousin who I have not seen in over twenty years. His parents had asked me to pick him up when he was released from his last prison stay. I did so. One would think he would have been appreciative of my efforts but no, he was as mean and crude as ever."

She then went on to tell the Chief in great detail, what Valerie and Rich had undergone in San Francisco.

"They are young and naïve, but they went too far when my daughter tried to do something nice for this bum who had attacked them. The ice cream cone bit was pure stupidity. But what most worried me was my daughter coming out of that entire event thinking she knew the man. We argued that one out for days,, but I could not dissuade her from that thought. Now she comes away from this past turmoil with the same belief and her description of that maniac. In particular it is his crazy blond hair, which much resembles mine, that has brought me to you."

The Chief just sat there listening and pondering over what he had just heard.

"How do you feel about it now and where is that cousin of yours now?"

Melissa thought for some time before answering.

"I could have been here to see you much sooner, but I had to give much thought to it before I did so. I'm beginning to think my daughter could be on to something. I remember when I was in my teens the kids at high school would call us the ugly twins. Certainly our hair color was absolutely the same color."

"And when did you last hear from him."

"Oh, I haven't heard from him in many, many years. I recall a phone call from his parents painfully telling us that he was back in prison for a ten year term, but I can't recall when we were told that. I suspect he has been out of jail for some time now but I am not certain of that."

The two just sat there deep in their own thoughts. It was Melissa who broke the deep thinking.

"Chief, for years that bastard seemed to look so much like me. I know who he is, and how bad a human being he can be. I also know that Valerie as a very young child was exposed to him and the arguments we had in the family about that terribly crazed human being. Please, talk to her. She could shed some information on the awful murder mystery that now besieges your town. More importantly, my daughter needs to talk to someone like you who can free her from the agony she is currently plagued with."

Chapter Thirty-Nine

That very next day Valerie, Rich, and Melissa sat with the Chief, his adjutant, the Mayor of Ashland, and two secretaries. They were in the main conference room which allowed them to televise the meeting.

Valerie had been prepped by her mother, so she was prepared to let out all she felt.

"They will all be on your side. Without you they have nothing to go on, but with you they may have a chance to resolve this mystery."

The Chief started the proceedings by thanking Valerie for coming forward.

"With you we might have a chance of finding the man who had assaulted you and killed your dear friend. This vilest of men must be found, and I intend to put forth every effort to do so."

With Rich tightly holding her hand she started quite slowly. Bit by bit, every inch of her story did come forth.

"What frightens me most is that for some reason I felt like I knew the man. He frightened me in San Francisco and terrified me in this beautiful cemetery of yours."

Rich joined in by laying out all of the events that occurred on both their trips to San Francisco and the walk to Tony's cabin.

Melissa joined in to repeat the story of her ill-fated cousin who was the personification of evil.

"He was a sick and infuriating child. I believe he was about twelve the first time he was arrested. He had gotten two eight year olds and tempted them to take a run with him through the nearby woods. In the deepest part of the woods he bound them up and then set their clothes on fire. He raced off leaving the two boys to a certain horrific death. Fortunately, an adult stumbled upon the two bound children within moments and saved them."

Melissa went on telling of the boys identifying Irvine as their torturer which led to a series of sessions with a psychologist. She continued with further details of her cousin. Fortunately, she had not seen him in years. He was a few years older than her which placed him in his early fifties. She described his physical appearance as best as she could and noting that his name was Irvine Crawford and that he resembled both herself and Irvine's dad.

She handed an old photo to the Chief which she said was the photo of the father of the man who had committed the terrible crime in Ashland.

"But tell me Mrs. Crawford didn't your daughter, in describing the first man who questioned her, say that she could hardly see him before he knocked her cold?"

"My daughter says it is not the exact resemblance of

the man who attacked her both in San Francisco and in Ashland but she feels that it is close."

The Chief immediately wired the photo to his counterpart in Frisco who called back to say, "Yes, that is a good shot. He's the guy we've had locked up any number of times, but all we could charge him for was being a major pain in the ass. I wish I could tell you that we'll have him for you, but we don't have a clue as to where he is now."

Melissa added that her current image of the man was based on the fact that she had last seen the man's father at about the same age that Irvine would be now. In some detail she described what a horror the boy and man were. How he nearly destroyed the good family he was raised in and, indeed, the Crawford's had long since disowned him.

"He had two brothers and one sister all of whom have never been anything but great people. I can't imagine where this man called Irvine came from. He was a horror from the very first. My goodness when he was only fourteen he almost burnt down their home. He was accused of raping a little girl when he was fifteen and was in and out of jail for most of his life."

She slumped back in her chair and in a very tired voice spoke of the death of Irvine's parents.

"He was never more than a petty criminal who had a wickedness that coursed through is body. That horror of that child drove his parents mad. No, that would have been easy. He drove them sick. Real sick! They were both dead before they were sixty."

Chapter Forty

shland, Oregon, was astir. Even their beloved Oregon Shakespeare Festival received its share of abuse. The less intellectual of its population started rumors that its sloppy hiring practices had brought a mad killer into its midst.

The papers, the radio stations, the local TV and the schools had serious articles, programs and lectures emphasizing the fact that this was not an Ashland affliction but an incursion of a lone madman that had brought this sin into their city.

The articles angered most who had read of this horrid killing. Most of all they hated the words that soon spread comparing the death that had occurred in 1858 to this current killing. Some soon heard words that depicted Ashland as a home for killers.

Valerie had the most serious guilt siege. She was certain that she had somehow lured that madman into town. She was undoubtedly related to the man who had killed her favorite friend. She found it trying to be with anyone other than her mother or Rich. Even Tim was difficult for her to tolerate,

She plagued herself with suspicions that all the horrors that had fallen on this town were caused by her and her alone.

At Rich's forcing, Valerie's mother said she had to go home to her husband and family. It took a great deal of effort to finally convince Val that she should join her mother in a needed respite from Ashland.

Tim was rather annoyed that Valerie and her Mom, whom he had grown quite fond, of and even his best friend Tony, had all left him.

"All I have left to talk to is you and you never buy me ice cream."

Rich had told Tim that Tony was off on a trip but that all four would soon be reunited. That explanation did nothing to appease Tim.

"Oh, he once told me that he might take a long trip but I never believed he would leave us. In fact he promised that he would take me with him. So, if he is on a trip now, why didn't he take me with him?"

There was no real response that Rich could come up with.

A strong despondency fell upon poor Tim. He so missed his almost daily talks with Tony.

"I miss him so much and the stories he used to tell us. Do you think he will ever come back?"

"Of course he will. I think he is missing you as much as you are missing him. He will be back soon and he will have a million more stories to tell us about. I was talking with him just before he left and he told me all about the KKK story that he was going to tell you. Do you remember him speaking of that and what troubles bad men can bring about?"

"No, but is it a good story?"

"It is a great one and kind of reminds me of the crazy things you hear going on in town today. If you like, I'll tell you what he told me."

"Wow. That's great. And when he gets back and tries to tell me the story I'll tell it to him and he will be so surprised that I already know his story, and he won't know how I got to know it. Promise me you won't tell him."

"You got it, bro. I'll never tell him a word about it"

With that Rich turned away from his brother. He did so for this was the worst case of his telling blatant lies to his brother. He also didn't want Tim to see the tears that were coursing down his cheeks.

He tried to get into the KKK story, but it was too difficult to even try to emulate Tony. His entire world had been turned upside down.

Tim sat beneath him and one could see the expectancy mount in his face. Even a hint of a smile started breaking through.

"Okay Rich, I'm ready to hear Tony's KKK story."

"And I'm ready to tell it to you but as you know I'm not as good a story teller as Tony is. Why don't we take a break then have some dinner. When we are done with the dishes I'll call Tony and get him to tell me the story once again. And when I've stopped talking with him I'll put him on the phone with you."

"Gee Rich you know I don't like talking on the phone."

"Oh darn. All right, let's postpone the call. But I promise I will try to do as good a job as Tony would. Does that sound okay to you?"

Tim gave him a big hug as he shouted "I don't like you. I've never liked you but, I've always loved you."

With that Rich picked Tim up, gave him several gentle punches and carried him to his bedroom. He then flung Tim onto his bed while shouting out, "You have five minutes to get to sleep before I beat the breath out of you."

Chapter Forty-One

*I*t was but one day later that Tim woke and burst into tears. Rich knew there was only one thing that could bring on that amount of tears. Tim was in despair over Tony leaving without saying one word to him.

Rich leaped across the rooms and grabbed the brother he loved so much and started kissing and spinning him to and fro while telling the boy that so many good things were going to happen real soon.

He finally gained his brother's interest when he told the biggest lie he had ever offered the boy.

"Now, listen up and stop crying. I just got a letter from Tony, and last night, after you fell asleep, he called me to explain what he was doing and where he was. As usual his timing is perfect. I told him about my wanting to tell you the Ku Klux Klan story and he gave me all I needed to know. So, why don't we get dressed, have breakfast and go up the mountain, and I'll tell you all about those very bad men."

Tim jumped out of his bed and started getting dressed. It was far from a perfect job, as trying to eat while tying his shoelaces was a monumental job to him. He started heading for the front door with a sandwich in one hand as the other hand fussed with the untied shoe.

"Hold off big guy. First get your big ass into the bathroom. Brush your teeth, wash your face and comb your hair. Then we will worry about food and shoes. Once we accomplish that we are going to hike up the mountain across the street and find a spot near Tony's house. I'm not as good a story teller as Tony is and this KKK story is a doozy, so if I confuse you, tell me so, and I'll try to do a better job of it. Are you sure you can handle a story about some very bad people?"

"Sure I can, and I'll tell you just like you tell me when I do a good job or when you tell me when I do a bad job.

"Well that is something like it, but you are really a good person almost all of the time. I'm talking about people who are bad most of the time."

They sat down next to a tree that was special to Tony. Rich started to talk as simply as he could about the Civil War. He explained how difficult the war had been and how much havoc it had wreaked on people from both the North and the South.

Tim just stared at Rich his eyes never leaving Rich's face as he smiled contentedly at every word that came from his brother's mouth.

Rich started talking about the differences between the two sides.

"The northern part of our country believed in freedom for all and the southern part of the country believed all black people should be slaves. Each side hated the other because of their feelings about slavery. Do you understand that?"

"I'm not sure. What's a war and what's a slavery?"

"A war is where one group of people disagree with another group of people, so they form an army and send them out to kill the people who believe differently from them. Of course the other side puts together their army and the two armies fight what is called a war. Many men on each side are killed or seriously wounded. That is called a war. Slavery is when a person is owned by another person and has to do whatever his owner says. He is called a slave. If he doesn't do it exactly right, the owner could even kill him. So doing that is called slavery. Do you get it? "

"I wouldn't like being a slave. You tell me to do a lot of things, and mostly I don't do it right, but you never hate me for what I do or do not do. You just tell me how to do it right."

"Yes, but we love each other. I could never hate you, and I am sure you could never hate me."

With that he grasped both of Tim's hands and whispered into Tim's ears, "Just know that I love you so much too. I wake up each morning loving you, and I go to sleep smiling to myself about you.

He then asked Tim to join him by saying 'Love Matters.' They must have repeated the words over twenty times before Rich kissed his brother on the forehead and Tim, in turn kissed his brother.

"But how can people who live in the same country hate a guy who may live next door to him?"

"As usual, Tim, you've hit the biggest problem right on the nose.

"Rich, I'm lost. It's like I live on one street and I hate the people who live on the next street. That doesn't make any sense."

"I sure agree with you, but each side felt so strongly about their position that the only way they could resolve the problem was to start a war."

"Again, what's a war?"

"You know you always ask the toughest questions but here goes. First off, war is crazy. Even thinking of starting a war is the wackiest thing that man has ever done, and he has done it over and over again throughout the history of the world. So I try to kill you and all your believers and, of course, you try to kill as many of my believers as possible, and that's war."

"I still don't know what war is."

"Well just imagine that you and I are arguing about something. We both think we are the right ones. So to prove that we are the right ones, each of us gets all the men we know and arm them with guns and bombs so that they can kill those who believe otherwise. Many men on both sides are killed in the ensuing battles. That is what is called a war."

"That sounds real dumb to me."

"You are right on, but when one side says 'I'm right' and the other side says 'I'm right,' each side tries to kill off as many of the people who don't believe their way."

"Are you saying that I must kill you if I don't like what you believe in?"

"I know that sounds stupid but, yes, that's a war. Each side tries to kill off the most men, and when they can't take any more of the killing, they are the losers and the other side is the winner."

"That's stupid. Can't they just pick a winner and then not have to kill so many people?"

"That, my man, is a brilliant statement you have just said. But as long as there have been men on this earth of ours, the men have spent a bulk of the time killing each other. In this case, so many soldiers were killed on both sides in that stupid war that it nearly ruined all of the United States. The people of the South realized that their hatred was never going to stop the North from winning this war so they conceded victory to them. What do you think the South kept in their hearts?"

"Hey that's too tough a question."

"I guess you are right. Here's a clue. The people from the South hated their Northern enemies so much they never forgave them."

"I got it, Rich. Both sides kept hate in their hearts for the other side, as both sides wept for all their boys who had been killed."

Tim stared blankly at his brother, for he didn't have a clue as to what next happened.

"I don't blame you for not knowing what was yet to come. There was so much disaster accompanying the end of the war that they kept looking for something that would say they were still right in their hatred."

"So what did happen?"

"Well, people in the South kept looking for ways to let the world know of their continuing hatred for the North. It is said that in Pulaski, Tennessee, which is a city in the South, six Southern officers formed a group that called itself the Ku Klux Klan. So far as I know, the words are based on Greek words but have no other meaning. They, as a group, hated everything about the end of the war. At first, the Klan, its popular name, just kept hatred alive to justify what they so strongly believed. Their intention was to renew the war that had just ended."

"Rich that seems real dumb to me."

"It was more than dumb. They slowly began to realize that they were small in numbers and would never change the results of the war so they started spreading another kind of hatred."

Rich went on telling how the KKK started changing from just a small bunch of men meeting to discuss the good old days into an aggressive bunch trying to incite a new kind of war. The new message that Klan members shouted out most ferociously was their belief that every Freedman, Catholic, Jew, Black, Non-believing White, and any others who didn't endorse their hateful ways was doomed to a deserved and violent death.

Tim had to break into Rich's talk.

"Rich, I'm sorry but I'm confused and worried. Those people who hate so much. Do they hate us?"

"They would have to hate us because we do not believe as they do. But that is not something to worry about. They lost the war and just about everything they propose. Most Americans hate and distrust Klan members. They have been around for over one hundred and fifty years, and they are as sad a group of miscreants as has ever existed. Yes, there are still Klan groups existing in our country, but they are but a tiny number which are detested by almost all of America."

Tim was shaking and clutching his arms around himself. "I don't like this story. It scares me. Don't tell me anymore."

"No, Tim. You have to see one other thing. It is a photograph that was taken many years ago. The Klan thought they looked grand and noble in their official garb which was white sheets that cover everything from the top of their heads to the bottom of their shoes. Some Ashland local Klan members decided to stage a parade that would bring forth many new members from Ashland folk who endorsed the Klan. This was way back in Ninety Hundred and Twenty One."

"Okay Rich. Let me see that picture hear the rest about these bad people and then I don't want to hear anything else about those crazy Klan people."

Rich opened an envelope which he had put together for Tim to see. The envelope contained only a shot of Klan members walking through mid-town Ashland.

"Rich held the picture for Tim to look at. This shot was taken in mid-Ashland. They are garbed in their whites which was their official uniform. They gained less than six new members, and the city government informed the Klan leaders that they had their first and last parade that would ever be allowed in Ashland."

Tim studied the photo. He counted the marchers and then the viewers. He lost count each time he did so and finally said. "I guess some people might like the picture, but it didn't do anything to me."

He then took the picture out of Rich's hands and pinned it on the wall and stared deeply at it.

He finally turned to Rich saying "You know something Rich, there is not one thing in this picture that would make me want to be one of them."

Then, proceeding without a word being spoken, Tim tore it to shreds.

Rich was never prouder of his brother.

Chapter Forty-Two

Once Irvine drove out of Ashland, which was but minutes after sending those bullets into Tony's chest, he realized that he had to high tail it as fast as possible out of Oregon.

Getting away from the dangers facing him dominated Irvine's every thought. Slowly a plan evolved that seemed to make sense. He must get as far away as possible from this area. No, just fleeing to another state was not far enough. He must get to Canada or better still to Alaska.

Not only was that a good plan, but he had the contacts to make it work.

He drove as rapidly as he could to meet with a man in Seattle who could save his ass by printing the one item he most needed. Be it fraudulent corporate papers or a U.S. passport, this guy could deliver a perfect replica of same. The cost would vary from job to job. Going in he knew a passport would be among the most costly of items to deliver.

Irvine reached Seattle in but a few hours. It took but a few hours more to locate the one man who could create the item he most needed. Early the next morning he pocketed a fresh and perfect passport. He was now James Mitchell from Seattle, Washington. He paid for this vital item by coupling the money he had stolen from Valerie with what he had gained in selling the car he had used in Ashland. Within hours he had jump started and then stolen yet another small car.

The next day he donned a tired looking baseball cap as he easily passed into Canada. His new passport had stood him in good stead as he headed for Vancouver. He could hardly contain himself as he awaited his meeting up with two former fellow prisoners.

The three were all imprisoned for crimes done in the U.S., although his new friends were born in Vancouver, Canada. It was an odd place to develop a strong friendship.

They had started their life of crime as small time hoodlums in southern Canada, but early on looked to the U.S. for bigger prospects and soon headed south.

Their downfall occurred in Pennsylvania where they were caught after committing the sloppiest robbery conceivable. A ten year sentence was easy to handle, as they quickly beat every fellow prisoner who challenged their dominance.

Their reputation as being even tougher than they looked spread quickly. The older one was called 'The Boss' by one and all, because he had quickly beaten the hell out of many a fellow prisoner. That action led to his silent rule over his fellow prisoners. If you wanted to beat the hell out of an inmate fellow you had better clear it with Boss before proceeding.

The younger one was called 'Smashim.' Do something the Boss didn't approve of and 'Smashim' would beat the hell out of the one thus honored.

Even the warden called them by those 'prison- given' names. They loved their titles and swore that they would keep those names whether or not they were in prison.

Their jail stint had been rather long before Irvine had arrived in the same cell block. He looked up to them as leaders and guides on how to stay alive in this hellish existence.

Boss got out one year prior to Smashim, but both had told Irvine to get up to Vancouver where they would soon be setting up a new profit-making scam.

"We sure could fit in someone as crazy as you."

Arriving in Vancouver, Irvine didn't take much time to find his ex-jail mates. He sought out the crudest looking bar and watched as an equally cruddy bunch of men kept flowing in and out. He stood outside the bar for several hours and proved this was the place to pose his questions when one hooker after the other started flowing into the bar.

He followed them in but carefully ignored them. Instead he walked to the bar and slapped down a $20 bill while asking the bartender if he knew about two very tough gentlemen who didn't take shit from no one.

The bartender pocketed the twenty and walked away without speaking a word.

A half-hour later, and though still without a drink, the bartender beckoned him to the end of the bar. They walked but a few steps when the bartender turned to Irvine and without saying a word gave him a serious shove that propelled him into a darkened room. The shove had included a thorough frisking of Irvine.

As he turned into the room a small light was turned on. Still without speaking a word the bar man shoved Irvine further into the empty room and then slammed the door shut leaving Irvine alone in the barely lit room.

Irvine stood in the center of the room patiently waiting. Some moments passed and then a voice shouted out, "Hey you old Turd. How did you get out, and where the hell have you been for all these years?"

Chapter Forty-Three

The next weeks brought great pleasure to the three old friends. Mostly the bragging and boasting came from the Canadians. They asked nothing of Irvine. In fact they were overly generous to him. He was given free housing, a free tab at the bar, use of any of their hookers and never asked him to do anything that would aid their endeavors.

They far exaggerated their exploits, but there was enough truth in their claims that Irvine began to feel that he had to do some boasting of his own, so that they would think he could become a very important addition to their operations.

Finally, one afternoon the three were sitting quietly in the bar when one of their lieutenants came tearing in. He pulled Boss aside and whispering feverishly related a tale of some rueful consequences.

Boss exploded with anger.

"It was a simple job. Can't anybody do anything right?"

Irvine had no idea as to what the foul up had been but felt that this was his opportunity to impress them with his talents.

"Hey, Boss, if you have any problems, why don't you turn them over to me and I can straighten them out right off."

Boss hardly looked at Irvine but told Smashim to get a couple of the boys together and go over to Pete's and beat the hell out of Pete's son. "Breaking an arm and a leg might be a good idea.'

Irvine continued pleading with Boss to let him be the one to clear up this little situation but nothing could stir Boss to get excited about having Irvine get involved with his business, Truth of the matter was that he had no serious belief in Irvine's ability to get anything done well.

"I've been free loading here for weeks now and that's not my style. Maybe you don't know enough about what I am capable of doing so let me tell my latest venture."

Boss kept fuming but did turn an ear to Irvine.

"You know when we first met I was the dumbest of the dumb. The cops dragged me in for the stupidest heist job ever. But I learned how to do things. Let me tell you of my latest gigs."

With that he started bragging of his past criminal exploits. Each deed was exaggerated far beyond its real venality.

Boss seemed to calm down as he showed interest in what Irvine was saying. This of course encouraged Irvine and he kept embellishing his past exploits.

"I had walked into a liquor store which was totally empty. I pushed my hand into my coat pocket and told the guy behind the pocket that I wanted all the money in the cash register. I wriggled my hand in what was, of course, an empty pocket. I told him if he didn't start moving a lot faster there would be a lot of blood soon pouring from him. I thought the guy was so scared that he was going to have a heart attack."

Irvine kept describing how the man kept slowly backing towards the register, while never taking his eyes off of Irvine.

"All of a sudden I felt a gun pointed into the back of my head. What that bum was doing as he backed away from me was heading towards a button that he finally got to and pushed. That told his partner in the back of the store what was happening up front."

Boss and all the others broke out in hysterical laughter.

"Yeah, I now can laugh it off but thank goodness I didn't have a rod on me. That could have gotten me ten years, but it only got me a few years for attempted robbery. When I got out of the clink, I had the rest of my future laid out. Here's what I did. First off, I let myself look like an aging old nut case."

Boss was by now practically hysterical. He very laughingly asked Irvine if he could tell them more about his skills. Unfortunately, all the braggadocio he produced yielded only a great despair from Boss and turned the Bosses men into a wild group, hilariously leading Irvine into ever more ridiculous exploits that were obviously total fiction.

"Hey, Boss, isn't that just what we need?"

Irvine knew he was being mocked and tried again to reach them using all of the whole adventure that had started in San Francisco. He was very dramatic in his presentation and his words scored very heavily with all of his listeners. He explained what directed him to Ashland and then segued into the vicious murder he had committed all in the room quieted.

Boss very quietly asked, "Are you saying that you shot and killed some guy who wasn't carrying anything more than his fists?"

Irvine replied that he could not have cared less. He had to get rid of that intruder and get the hell out of there.

Those were not the words that Boss wanted to hear. He slowly rose and walked towards Irvine.

"You just killed a man, and then you come to my house to hang out? What kind of a miserable little bastard are you? You are without a doubt being looked for by every cop in Northern U.S as well as Southern Canada, and you bring your filthy life into my life. That wasn't a very nice thing to do?"

Fury was printed all over Bosses face. He was glaring at a suddenly frightened Irvine who started backing away from the Boss, who grew closer and closer to Irvine. Slowly he extended his hands as his fingers tied themselves around Irvine's throat.

Irvine started slashing out fiercely, but Smashim hit him full force in the middle of his face. His nose was totally smashed. Bosses fingers grew tighter and tighter. With every word that Irvine tried to spit out, the fingers grew more rigid and the coughing grew more and more intense. Suddenly everything stopped for Irvine.

"Get this piece of shit the hell out here. He is beginning to stink up this room. Take him up to Vancouver and throw him and all that he brought here with him, and that includes that pitiful car, into the river. Make sure he and everything about him sinks into the water so that they never can come up again."

Now totally calm he turned away from what he had just done.

As he was about to exit the room he quietly turned around and rather quietly said, "That piece of garbage was never here."

No one ever heard of the demise of the killer of Tony.

Chapter Forty-Four

Through the years murders being committed in Ashland were extremely rare and rarely stirred interest in the citizens of the city. Yes they did read and reread a book about the history of Ashland, for it seemed to be mandatory reading for all.

Current citizens started to once again pick up the book so as to compare the earlier killing to the one that had just occurred. This also unsolved mystery led to as few answers as did the first killing. People began to compare the earlier killing to the one that had just stained their wonderful city.

The first killing was of a good friend who was revered by most citizens of Ashland. This very recent slaying was of a man who was almost equally treasured by the current citizens of the city. Yes, the city had grown much between the two murders, but today's homicide caused even greater grief to spread through the town.

Ashland tried to rise to the occasion. It was if every resident of Ashland had roles to play in this very trying theatre piece called 'Keep Everyone Happy.' But when these locals gathered together they had only one narrative to pursue, "How could this have happened yet again in our wonderful city?"

Valerie was a basket case. She never shed the feeling that all was her fault. It totally changed an ebullient beautiful young woman into a sad soul that rarely spoke. Sulking was her major occupation and what had been a torrid love affair between her and Rich became merely a relationship with limited conversations which mostly dwelt on keeping Valerie happy.

Rich, Tim and Valerie's Mom were the only ones who hardly changed. Rich still got a charge from mounting the stage and acting his heart out, while Melissa Crawford remained the only person her daughter, Valerie, could so much as talk to.

Tim, of course, was Tim.

Valerie's on stage performances seemed to remain almost up to par but all in the cast, particularly Rich, knew that most of the fire Valerie usually brought to every role she presented had become a tepid read through.

A week of this was enough to draw Melissa and Rich together.

"Melissa, we can't let this go on much further. The Festival is being quite nice, but sooner or later they will have to force Valerie to leave the company. It will be terrible for her to be dropped from the company. She has got to be the one who asks for a leave. That will allow her to come back to open arms next season."

Melissa agreed. "I know you are right in everything you say but that little lady will never quit anything. We must come up with an alternate plan that forces her to do what we want her to do, and I think I have an idea that could work."

Just before the next day's matinee, Valerie came to Rich looking as if someone had been beating on her for the past twenty-four hours.

"What the hell has happened to you?"

"Mom woke this morning and took her own temperature and it was quite high. She had gone to bed early saying that she wasn't feeling too well and she hardly slept a moment all night. I'm going to see Walt right now and tell him of my problem. I promise he will let me go off for as long as Mom needs me."

Within the hour, Rich and Val barged into Walt's office. As usual he commanded the conversation.

"Well it's about time you two decided to let me into your lives. What is it that you are suffering from now? No, forget that sentence. I believe I know the trauma that is hammering at you. What you need now is to get away from here and breathe some fresh air."

For many minutes, they merely stared at the artistic director of the Festival. Then Valerie jettisoned her fear of this man and jumped into his extended arms.

The kisses she covered him with brought Walt and Rich the biggest smiles that each had ever worn. Walt gently pushed her off while pretending to be annoyed.

"You are ruining my reputation as a self-centered egoist. Give me one more kiss like that, and I may have to ask you to marry me. Now get out of this office and come back whenever you care to. Val, you can take off whenever you care to and, Rich, staying or going is your decision

This time both Valerie and Rich covered Walt with kisses as they dashed out. He watched them tear out of his office as his heart began to cry out. He hurt for these ultra-talented beings who had earned deserved acclaim from all and not the horror they were living through. He knew that Valerie would be the only one to leave and he was pleased with that.

Chapter Forty-Five

Much as they loved one another, Valerie and Rich spent many an hour arguing the feasibility of both going east to take care of Melissa.

Valerie had argued that they should all remain in Ashland. Rich thought the only way to get her mother healthy and with some speed was to take her back to the environment she knew and loved. Melissa cast the deciding vote.

"Look, I don't need either of you to take care of me. Valerie you take me back into my own house and give me a few days to get settled and then you come back here to help Rich take care of Tim, and by then, I will be as healthy as can be. That's all I'll need."

"Mom, I've always known you were stubborn but I never thought you were stupid. You are one sick woman. Will you get well? I certainly hope so. Let Rich and me take you home and spend as much time with you as needed."

"Me, the stubborn one? The word was coined for you my darling child. And what's this about Rich joining this expedition to save Momma? No way, I'm about to ruin either of your careers. Yes, I need Valerie for a short time, and I will miss scolding Rich, but I'll soon get over that. Tim needs him more than I do. So let this old woman have her way. Besides, I want to be as mean and cranky as is possible without worrying if it is bothering anyone."

Thus Melissa almost immediately shot down the proud words offered up, as she burst into the worst hacking cough she had ever had. They all knew that Valerie would not be back in Ashland for a long time. Two days later, Rich and Tim waved goodbye to their beloved women.

As he often did, it was Tim who came up with the words that most identified what had happened to all of them. Having witnessed Melissa's and Valerie's takeoff he took Rich's arm and with a sad voice told his brother.

"You know, Rich, this is a dumb world. First Tony has to go away. Now I lose Valerie and her Mom who I really like. The way things are going I expect you to take off any time now. I guess I'll have to find a place to go to where I can find a friend that will stay with me."

Chapter Forty-Six

K nowing that Tony was one of Rich's and Tim's best friend and learning of Valerie and her mother having left them stranded everybody in the company adopted the two waifs. Thus hardly a night went by that they weren't invited out for dinner at a great restaurant or to the home of one or another killer chefs in the company where a meal fit for Royalty was prepared.

By far the biggest gift to come to Rich was from the Festival's always busy artistic director, Walt Somers, who had sent word to Rich to be in his office at 9:00 a.m. the following morning. Rich got there five minutes early and was greeted with a huge hug. It was not followed with any small talk.

"Rich, I know you love the roles you have this season and you are performing them beyond perfection, but as of right now I'm cutting you from both plays. As a matter of fact, I want you and Tim to leave Ashland as soon as feasible."

A stunned Rich garbled out something like "I don't

think I heard you correctly. What I heard makes no sense whatsoever. Why in the name of hell would you fire me for playing a role so well?"

"This has nothing to do with your ability. It has everything to do with what a board member and one of his employees told me last night. In essence if what they tell me is true you are in terrible danger."

Walt kept tapping his pencil on his desk. He looked everywhere in the room but at Rich. Finally he rose, tossed the pencil on his desk, as he approached the angry young man standing opposite of him.

"I don't know if you noticed that there were several policemen in front of your building this morning?"

Rich had noticed and agreed by strongly shaking his head.

"Well they are there now on a 24 hour basis. I have been told that there is fear that you or Tim might be in serious danger. I'm about to tell you what may be the craziest words I have ever uttered, but they are totally relevant."

He went on to blurt out as quickly as he could what the Chief of Police had advised him the previous evening.

"He told me to get you and Tim the hell out of town as soon as possible.

"Walt you are scaring me silly. Did I hear that correctly?"
Walt nodded his head.

Rich quietly asked what had prompted those words.
He then carefully and slowly related the following.

"The chief told me that Tony had ten men working for him at the cemetery. Their job was to keep it neat and clean and safe for the folk visiting their deceased relatives. It is a very low paying job and therefore the people working for

Tony were not exactly the elite of the working class. But they did share one thing. They all loved Tony for being the nicest and most caring boss any of them had ever worked for."

"What has all of that got to do with me…with my life?"

Walt dropped his 'Nice Uncle' attitude and launched into Rich.

"Chief swore to me that what I am about to tell you is pure gospel. It seems that one of his sergeants, James Wingate, has an older brother who was a member of Tony's crew. That brother, who is a bit of a daft one, came to his younger brother who had the good sense to bring that message on to the chief,"

"Well what the hell has that got to do with me?"

Walt in an almost an inaudible voice said, "Rich if I don't get you out of town real soon some crazy people might try to kill you. "

Rich started to laugh. The laughter became almost hysterical as he determined that those words meant no sense whatsoever.

"What I really can't understand is why a guy as busy as you would waste his precious time on such a stupid story."

Walt kept shaking his head as he looked at Rich chortling away. Finally, shaking his head and almost shouting he said, "No Rich, this is not some silly garbage. Tony's crew are going through town talking about how you hated Tony because he was always showing you up.

One of the men screamed out that Rich was pissed at Tony because, as everybody knew, Tony had been regularly putting it to Rich's lady friend.

"Walt, that can't be true. One day Tony took Tim and me to an 8:00 a.m. meeting with that bunch. He introduced us by telling them that he loved the two of us despite our being a couple of citified sissies. One of the men jumped up shouting out something about how his fellow workers loved Tony more than he loved these two sissies. He went on to say Tony was the only man who showed them respect and loved them. And then, all the other men jointly shouted out, "Tony was da best and we love the hell out of him."

Walt cut him off by relating that a bunch of upper class Ashland men met with Tony's crew, trying to see if they could learn something from Tony's crew. What scared the hell out of Walt was that many of the so called elitists at that meeting told him that both workers and elitist, agreed that Rich could have been the killer of their much loved friend.

Chapter Forty-Seven

$\mathcal{R}$ ich and Tim decided not to leave town but willingly accepted the Police Chief's offer of twenty-four hour protection. Of much more importance, they were excited about a proposed meeting which would bring them face to face with their accusers. Both sides agreed that was a wise idea.

They met in late afternoon in the Chief's office. All that gathered in that crowded room were in varied moods. Tony's men were both scared silly and angry as hell. The so called elite group was furious for being ordered to attend this meeting. At Rich's request, Tim was not invited to the meeting.

The Chief started the meeting off strongly.

"Thank you all for being on time. We have to clear something up that could have been disastrous but seeing you all here I know we can put our minds and energies to work to straighten out this mess.

With that he turned to Rich and said, "Rich, it's all yours. Tell us whatever you want to but remember, there isn't a criminal in this room, only people who loved Tony."

Rich stood up and quietly walked to each man in the room and offered his hand in greeting.

"For those of you who do not know my brother, Tim, he has had a dreadful mental disease since birth. But he loves just about everyone he knows. Far and away his favorite was Tony who, in turn, fell in love with my troubled brother. He did so because he understood Tim's problems and Tim worshipped Tony. They would meet at least once every day, and most days I was part of their sessions. Tony taught us everything about what makes a cemetery click and, more importantly, what makes a man click. It took no time at all for me to fall in love with Tony. The third member of our class was Valerie, who I hope will become my wife later this year. I am the luckiest man in the world because she loves me. Valerie is currently out of town taking care of her very ill mother. When she returns she will get to meet all of you, and I guarantee you will fall in love with her."

He went on by telling of her love for his brother and that yes, Valerie also loved Tony.

'That was her way. Look for people you can deeply love and forget all the others. We all were fortunate to have Tony as a part of our lives. He taught us about loving your fellow man. He adored life and took much time expressing what was good about people and the world we lived in. He was a gift to us that we shall always treasure. Each day I thank Tony for teaching me how lucky I am to have been a part of the world he so loved. To think that I or any of my family would harm Tony in any manner is pure idiocy."

He paused for several minutes as tears began to flow down his face. He looked sternly at the group. He wiped is face and then asked the men in a fierce tone.

"I tell you all of this, so that you realize neither of us could even think of harming Tony in any manner and that it is of great moment that every effort is put forth to find the monster who could find any rational for killing a man like Tony?

He then went on to say that he and all in his family would miss Tony for every day they remained alive.

For the longest period there was no response to what Rich had said. A great period of time passed before anyone else in the room uttered a word.

Ralph Walters, the most loud-mouthed member of Tony's crew rose to his feet. Tears were streaming down his face. At first he stood with his face fallen limp on his chest. Finally the words slowly came forth.

"I was so mad at our boss man being killed that I wanted to kill someone to get even for what they took away from me. Nobody has ever been as kind to me as Tony was and I will love him forever."

It took a while for him to continue speaking to this group.

"All of us will always miss Tony. He made us better men. I speak for all of our crew when I take back the terrible words we spoke about you, Rich. I am sure you are hurting as much as we are."

He turned and was about to sit in his chair when he stopped and turned back to the others.

"All of us guys have also agreed to donate all of our pay that we get for this month's work. It may not be a lot of money, but it sure is going to be tough on all of us to do so."

He sheepishly looked across at the others in the room. 'We don't have a lot money so all we want is that somewhere a sign is posted that says how much we loved that guy called Tony.

He walked to where Rich was sitting and they both embraced. There was not a dry eye in the room and that included the Police Chief.

Strangely enough none of the elite group had the balls to stand up and offer a word. They just sat there waiting for someone to say the words that would allow them to leave this dreadful meeting and get back to the more important matters they had to attend to.

Finally, the Police Chief rose and in the strongest of words offered his thoughts on how fortunate they all had been to have known Tony.

"This little town of ours should be shouting out to the world of our home-grown hero. Let us honor that man. City Council will soon be starting to put together a fund to honor Tony D'Angelo and the marvelous work he has done for all of us. Ralph, we will start that fund with the donation from those who have the least ability to do so."

At this point he promised one and all that his department would never stop working to find the perpetrators of this hideous crime.

The lone woman at this meeting sat with the work crew. She was the wife of one of the workers. As soon as the Chief sat down her strident voice burst forth.

"And we expect your contribution to be the same as we are giving. I repeat what my husband said. We are going to give all the money that we earn in a month of hard work. We expect the same from you. Hear me when I say all the money that you earn this next month. We are counting on you.

No one raised their voice in argument to that statement.

The Police Chief ended the meeting as he said "We will expect your checks to be in our hands before we release the news and names of the people who attended this meeting."

Several of the elitists immediately pulled out their check books and started scribbling away.

The Chief continued by saying that they must use that money raised for a cause the Tony would have approved of. Within minutes, all agreed that Tony most enjoyed doing work for the young.

It was Rich who suggested that the money raised should be used for young people who had somehow or other fallen into trouble.

"Let's teach them how to love rather than hate."

In minutes they created a foundation dedicated to improving the lives of Ashland's young people. The wealthier folk assured all that they would see to it that said foundation was always properly funded.

Chapter Forty-Eight

Rich and Valerie normally conversed by phone at least three or four times a day, so it was not abnormal for him to pick up the phone without a second thought. But calling her only two hours after their ten a.m. chat was rather unusual.

His first question to her on each call was usually, "How's my wicked lady doing?" but this call went right to all that he had gone through this morning.

"What was most marvelous about it all is that it mattered not if you were a rich man or a hard working guy earning barely enough money to exist, you contributed as best as you could."

After a rather long pause Valerie still hardly responded, which was most unusual for the biggest talker in Oregon. She did eventually tell him that her Mom was feeling a bit better and she would talk with him early that evening. She never brought up a word about what he had told her. He was more than puzzled by her lack of interest in what seemed to him was important information.

Later that evening Rich and Tim were finishing their dinner. Usually after dinner Rich jumped into some easy stretching exercises, vocalized for about five minutes and then raced off to the theatre. He was about to start same when it dawned on him that he was no longer a working actor. He was furious at everything in the world.

What maniac killed his friend Tony….Why had Walt taken him away from doing what he thrived on…Why the hell hadn't Valerie called as yet…And, what the devil was he going to do with the rest of his life.

Timing in one's life is often beyond bizarre. Certainly such a moment was about to explode on Rich. He and Tim started to clear the dinner table when the front door opened and a female voice shouted out, "You guys are the slowest and sloppiest workers I have ever seen."

As if choreographed, two dirty plates fell out of the hands of the brothers. The dishes fell crashing onto the floor. Rich and Tim spun around and there they espied their Valerie standing at the door with the biggest smile that had ever adorned her face.

She scrambled forward and instantly took Tim in her arms. She covered every part of his face with wet kisses and then turned to Rich. A hundred kisses later, a thousand hugs and squeezes and smiles that never stopped glowing on their faces and finally Valerie set her men down and told them that her Mom was really well and that while listening to Rich's telephone words this morning, she realized that he was the one in the family who really need her..

For Valerie it was nothing to pack a small bag, tell her mother that she was well enough to be on her own, to which her mother readily agreed, and speed to the airport to catch a plane that would land her in Medford at 7:30 pm and in Rich's arms one half hour later.

Chapter Forty-Nine

$\mathcal{V}$alerie hardly surprised herself by not wanting to dash back to acting with the Festival. What she really enjoyed doing was spending the days doing her favorite chore…THINKING.

It seemed she had spent half her life wondering if she had the acting skills to really make it in the big time. Yes, she had, to a certain extent, proven herself here in Ashland but the answer to whether or not she could cut it in New York or Los Angeles still eluded her.

At first she attributed her thinking about leaving theatre to the craziness of the life she had lived through over the past several months. She knew above all that she wanted to be with Rich. Keeping Tim happy had started as a way to keep Rich tied to her, but her affection and deep empathy for Tim had grown to where it was the most important activity in her day.

She was certain that Rich was the man for her. God knows she had played around with all sorts of guys but had never spent more than a month or two with any of those Lotharios.

Rich, on the other hand, never disappointed her. He had it all. He was as handsome as could be. He was considerate of everybody, be they male or female. He was the brightest man she had ever met, and his love for Tim could only have occurred in heaven.

There was little doubt in her mind that someday Rich would become a major star on Broadway, in Films and TV. There wasn't a man in the world who didn't admire Rich, and there wasn't a woman in the world who didn't try to hit on him.

Could she help in getting him there, or would her personal needs become an obstacle in his path to stardom?

For Valerie, Rich and Tim the next morning meant it was time to once again pay tribute to Tony. They packed a little picnic and hied up to the cabin. This trip was not to spend the morning worshiping the memory of Tony but to thank him for the joy he had brought them.

Valerie dug in first with Tim watching her closely as she took her first bite into the sandwich Tim had made.

"Tim, you are the greatest chef in the world. In fact you are such a marvelous cook and I loved this meal so much, I would like to marry you. Do I have a chance?"

At which point Rich jumped over to Valerie and fell to his knees. He kissed her foot and exclaimed, "You can't do that. He's too young for you and besides that you are going to marry me."

"Do you really want to marry me?"

"Yes. More, than anything else in the world."

Tim broke up this sweet moment by exclaiming that it would be great if they got married but could he marry her too?

Valerie offered another idea. Since three person marriages were rather illegal why don't they adopt him instead thereby making him their first child and then they could love him even more than they do now.

Tim considered this for a few seconds and then offered, "Hmm, aren't you my Mother and Father now."

Chapter Fifty

*V*alerie had not reported to the Festival that she was ready to come back to work. She got Rich to promise not to mention that she was even back in town.

The question that she was torturing herself with was an old story for young actresses. Does she have the chops to become a really fine actress, or was she just another pretty face who could only handle minor roles.

She didn't discuss this with Rich, as she knew he would never question anything about her. She knew that the best person to give her an honest answer was Walt Somers, the artistic director of the Festival. She knew he was the busiest man in town but despite that, and being the ballsiest gal in town, she picked up the phone and called Walt's secretary.

"If you can make it a short meeting he can see you late this afternoon. If not, then you will have to wait until next Tuesday at noon."

The following Tuesday at 11:45 Valerie stood at the secretary's office.

"Good that you came early. He will be back within a few moments so why don't you take a chair in his office now."

Valerie had hardly seated herself before Walt stormed in. He welcomed her with a tiny peck on her cheek plumped into his chair and shouted out a loud "Welcome Home."

"Thanks so much for seeing me. I've been struggling with something that is driving me crazy, and you are the one I need to help me resolve what is driving me mad."

"Valerie, I'm flattered that you came to me with what I am sure is a serious matter, but I'm just the artistic director of a regional theatre, not some brain filled with answers for everyone's problems."

She was nervous as could be and was folding and unfolding a handkerchief. The words seemed stuck in her mouth as she looked at him. It took several minutes before the words started pouring out.

"I guess I'm at a turning point in my life and I'm hoping you can help me make a decision that keeps eluding me."

He was about to reply with a pun about his needing her to help him in solving a dozen problems he was facing, but the desperate look on her face told him this was no time for levity.

"Since I, like every male in this company, am deeply in love with you, let's hear it. What's bugging you?"

She paused yet again, took a deep breath and then blurted out, "Do I have any chance of becoming a good actress, or am I just another pretty face that can get by only in certain easy roles?"

"Whoa. That is one hell of a question that needs a lot more information before it gets an answer. First off, unless your role is just to walk on and then off the stage there is no such thing as an easy role. I remember when I was just a young actor and was just terrified when I had to make my first appearance on stage and, for years, I never got over that fear. If that is your problem, do what I did – I would count to ten take a big breath and then fling myself on stage. But that's enough about me. First let me ask a few questions."

He then posed three questions. "Do you like acting? Is there something else you would rather be doing do or is there something else that is plaguing you?"

The answers came out quickly. "I adore acting, but all the roles I have performed have been meaningless bits of trivia. Let me tell you something that you don't know. When I was sixteen, I wrote a book entitled 'It Hurts to Be a Teenager.' I got a load of Kudos for it, but the best reward I got out of writing was the joy I got in the doing. I haven't written anything since then but the memory of those fun days has never left me. These past months have been a total hell, but I believe it has been a spur to my asking myself where I am going."

"And you and Rich? How are you two getting on?"

"If you promise not to tell anyone else, we are going to be married in a month or two. Probably it will be two months which will allow this season to end."

Walt uttered many hurrahs as he gave her a big hug.

"Your answer to my question will determine if I want to have another go at it here. No, that's not what I meant to say. I know that I want to be on this stage as it is where Rich will be. But that is no answer to what has been plaguing me. What I really want to know, is do I really have the goods to be an actress worthy of the craft?"

"And, I've got the answer. Do you have the technical

chops to make it? Yes, Yes, Yes. Do you have the balls to go on stage after stage night after night and wow the world with your performance each time is something nobody knows, and that includes you, baby. All I can suggest is that if at your age, you are already questioning yourself instead of shouting out 'Watch out Merrill Streep here I come,' you do have a problem. If at this stage of your life you can't say 'I'm the best' then I heartily suggest you get a job as the first female plumber in the U.S. of A."

He then rose from his chair and walked to her side of the desk.

"Let me make a confession to you. I finish each day at this job wondering how many times I have screwed up. But the next day I'm back at this desk with the hope that I do better today than I did all the prior days I've had this job. Why? Because I love the work I do, and I pray that one day I will indeed learn how to do it correctly. If you don't have that same feeling then get out of our business. You are one very talented and brainy young woman. I think that in your theater lifetime there wouldn't be a single role that you couldn't perform sensationally. Should you now venture out to try something different, I say go for It, sister.

He then pulled her up, kissed her lightly on both cheeks.

"But, I also think the day will come when you'll be back on stage. I'm going to watch your performance the first time you get back on the boards, and I bet you will be better in that performance than you have ever been. Now get out of here. I've got a million things to screw up today."

She threw her arms around Walt, and without another word, she crept out of his office.

Walt's secretary, who had heard every word of the meeting, kept her eyes glued to her desk thus allowing Valerie to silently creep away.

She realized that Walt had thrown the decision right back at her. Where she would go from here was still her decision to make. She felt she was close to making that decision but first she had to get Rich's opinion. Nothing could destroy their relationship so whatever he said would shape the decision she made.

Chapter Fifty-One

The next week was fraught with two notable events. The first was Valerie and Rich reappearing together in the little comedy they enjoyed doing, and the second was Valerie facing the fact that decision time had arrived. The enigma in her life still remained within her.

That night they had just returned home from their evening performance. She fussed with Tim and finally got him to go to bed.

Rich was about to put on his PJs when Valerie halted his efforts to do so.

"Rich, can I have a serious word with you?"

"No, I will not confess to having gone to bed with several young beauties while you were away, and I did have several lascivious ideas that led me to glorious night time dreams. How did your dreams progress?"

"Okay you oaf. Let me try again. I want to talk seriously with you. Are you up to that?"

"No, my love, I am more inclined to ripping your clothes

off and ravishing you. But as your tone of voice indicates, you are not on the same page as I am so let me hear it. What's bugging you?"

"I just need a simple answer to a simple question."

"Fire away. I am a whiz at replying to simple questions with simple answers."

She gave him a gentle whack on his head and then asked how he felt about being an actor for the rest of his life.

"Come on, I love acting. Why would I ever stop doing it? Come on what do you really want to talk about?"

With that, she tried to tell him of her meeting with Walt, and what her decision was. It was not easy to get the words out. Three times she tried to tell him of what had transpired and that she thought she knew what had to be done. But each attempt ended with a bunch of garbled words. Finally she managed to blurt out.

"I've been thinking about changing what I do with my life."

"Does that include deciding not to marry me?"

"There is nothing in my life that I am surer of doing than marrying you and doing it as soon as possible."

"Well I don't understand what you mean when you talk of changing your life. Why don't you start all over again and then I might be able to get a clue as to what the hell you are trying to tell me."

That turned on the anger which was accompanied with a barrel-full of tears. It was not that Richard was mocking her but that she was not certain she would ever be able to get her thoughts into some ordinary speaking mode.

Once again she tried to tell of her meeting with Walt.

"He could not have been nicer and he was of real help in my coming up with the answer I needed. What do you think of that?"

"What do I think of what?"

"Gosh, you are slow. He told me that I was the only person, other than you, that could help make that decision."

Richard looked at her as if she was just recently let loose from an insane facility."

"Okay. Let me start over again. You met with Walt and asked him, now listen carefully, you asked him what?"

Valerie looked at him as if he were a mad man.

"For pity's sake, I just told you that I asked him what I should do with the rest of my life.

"Did I leave the room when you told that to me?"

"No, you were here through all I told you. What is the matter with you tonight?"

She looked at him as if she was looking at a crazed enemy, and Rich realized he had pushed her too far. His ever strong Valerie was about to completely collapse.

He took her in his arms and apologized for being such a boor.

"I'm sorry for being so stupid. Obviously, you have a problem and I am a nitwit. But I love you more than any man has ever loved a woman, so please give me another try at coming up with the answer that you are looking for, and when you are done, I've got something to tell you that I hope you will agree to."

She took much time before speaking and the words came out quite slowly.

"I am going through a terrible time."

She then paused yet again.

"Let me try again. I don't know what I want to do with the rest of my life. No, I mean the rest our life. I love act-ing, but am I really good enough to ever become a really fine actress? Am I willing to work as hard as I must just to become a better actress? Will I ever play roles that are really demanding? Do I have the chops to pull that off? Do I have the potential to be a real actress, or should I forget the theatre and look elsewhere for creative satisfaction?"

"Young lady there is no doubt in my mind but that you have a huge career awaiting you in theatre. But Walt is right when he says you are the only one who can make that decision. All I can offer is that you should get out of this silly game unless it totally captivates you. If it doesn't, try something else. If that 'new you' brings with it a happiness far beyond what theatre provides you, then get your beautiful ass the hell out of theatre. But the realization might dawn on you that you really like this game we play in preference with anything else."

Rich added a gentle kiss and then, with a tiny smile simply added: "As far as I am concerned, you can become a plumber or just a producer of a thousand babies. The only thing that matters is that you always stay with me. No matter what you or I do, we must remain together. I do have one change that I want to make. I don't want to wait for you to become my wife. I want to marry you on the last Monday of this Season. We'll invite everyone in the company to attend our glory day and the ceremony will be held in the Elizabethan Theatre. The only other item I must add is that Tim must be my best man."

They sat there holding hands but not another word was spoken. She slid further into his arms but before they fell asleep she, oh so quietly, whispered in his ear "I'm going back to writing."

She never knew whether or not he had heard a word of that prior to falling asleep.

Yes, he had fallen asleep but only after he decided not to continue on with this charade. She would make her own decision and whatever it was it would be the right one for her. He knew that if he became the best husband in the world all would be well for both of them. He knew he loved her and needed her as much as he needed a stage to emote on.

Not another word about the future work-life of Valerie was mentioned during the following weeks, which led to the last month of the Festival's 2016 Season. Walt had called her into his office and advised her that there were several roles available to her in the coming season; but with a flood of thanks and kisses, she turned them all down.

What she kept a secret from all was that within the next few months she would be going back to school to replenish her writing skills which, hopefully, would enable her to pick up her pen and start writing again. What was most exciting was that she had a dozen plots whirling around in her head. Without so much as bragging to Rich, she felt that each of the plots she had come up with could be the basis for several good books.

Rich was the only one who knew what she was about to embark on, and he was ever prouder of his soon to be wife for daring to take on that oh so challenging field.

What most thrilled him about her decision to go ahead was her ability to accept the odds of failure in this competitive field. Failing did not bother her one bit. Pushing herself into creating something of worth excited every bone in her body.

Each morning she would awaken and shout out loud, "If I fail with my first book, I'll have the joy of writing my second or third or hundredth. Creating something new is all that matters."

Chapter Fifty-Two

During these last weeks of the Festival it seemed as if Rich and Valerie were too preoccupied with their doings to notice that Tim had been in almost constant tears about Tony never meeting with them any longer. The name and the man had all but vanished, and Tim missed him pitifully.

Fortunately, one morning Valerie awoke to the fact that she had been gabbing away to Tim but he had not replied to her even once. He just sat across the room with his face turned away from her.

She walked to him and turned his face up to her. He, oh so sadly, raised his face to her, and she saw that Tim's sweet face was filled with tears.

He did not have to utter a word for Val to know that he was grieving for Tony's absence. It awakened her to the fact that she must be more aggressive with Tim in bringing him back to being the joy he normally was.

She debated with herself about taking Tim up to Toby's cabin, but couldn't decide whether or not it would be good or bad to do so. It fell to Tim himself to make the decision. The very next evening Tim approached Rich and Val. At first he seemed a little fidgety but that disappeared quickly when he told them of a great dream he had.

"You know there is something I should tell you about. I had a dream last night and Tony was the star in it. He told me all about his traveling around and that I should stop crying so much about his being away. He promised me that he would restart the lessons as soon as he came back. I believe him. Why don't we take a trip up to his cabin and make sure it is okay for him when he gets back?"

What they had not been able to do for him, he had done for himself. The tears disappeared, and he was back to being their beloved Tim.

Val agreed wholeheartedly, and the very next morning they were off and up the hill without a taste of breakfast.

As they neared the cabin it was obvious that Tim was thinking more and more of Tony and the old days.

Valerie began to see a tear or two start to trickle down Tim's face. She worried that seeing the cabin without Tony there might have a negative effect on Tim. As they neared the cabin, she shouted out, "I am such a Ninny. I left his key in the house. I guess we will have to come back some other time."

Truth of the matter is that she held the key tucked in her pocket.

Tim glanced at the cabin and then muttered something about it being okay. "It doesn't matter. I'm sure I'll see him tomorrow down at my favorite spot."

Later that week she ran out of excuses about why she could not bring Tim up to the cabin. All was quiet with not a soul around to see her as she and Tim competed for who would reach the cabin first. What was of greatest importance to her was that Tim was having a fine time as they raced up the hill.

As he roared ahead of her she thought of her last conversation with Tony. It had taken place right on the same path she and Tim were now taking. At that time Tony had told her that he had found a set of papers that had disturbed him immensely.

He went on at some length about those papers, which numbered over fifteen sheets and that they were obviously written many years before he had found them. The writing was in a hand that had long since gone out of style and consequently was difficult to decipher. Tony had read it time and time again trying to determine the period of time that it had been written, but he never could decipher the date the pen was laid to paper.

"I tell you, Valerie, that those pages were written many years ago and they tell a sordid story. But it leaves me befuddled. That man had certainly written those words to a woman that he was desperately in love with. This was apparent in every sentence he wrote. But there was no indication that the love affair was in any manner reciprocal. Those papers are now in my cabin, and I will get them to you as soon as possible. When you read it yourself, you will believe what I have just said."

Ever the curious one, Valerie could hardly sustain herself in wondering how Tony had gotten the papers. It seemed as if he was reluctant about telling her all.

It took some prodding on her part before Tony added the remainder of the story.

"It is really a joke. One day an old friend of mine asked me to do a job for him. He took me to see the old house and an equally old storage building. He was fearful that both structures would soon be falling down of their own accord thereby ruining any profit he might get in the sale of them.

Actually, the job was a breeze. After a morning of hacking away at the older structure, it slowly began to fall apart on its own. I went on with the shoveling until I pushed over the last standing wall. Lying beneath one solid beam I found a heavily covered package stuffed into something like a pillowcase. The papers were soaked through and through.

I haven't yet read them totally, but I might do so tonight. I've got it all up in my cabin, and once I finish reading them I'd like you to take a gander at them."

By the next day he had read all of what had been hidden in those walls. That afternoon he corralled Valerie and told her that it was apparent that both of them should read the papers that Tony had discovered. Within moments they took off for Tony's cabin.

"The entire work is about this woman named Annette. The words revealed how deeply the writer was in love with her. But the shocking words also tell of the writer's murder of a man who is never fully identified."

Tony believed the murdered man was the fabled doctor who had been murdered in the middle of the previous century. He laboriously went through all of the facts and he was terrified by the words he had read.

"When you see the papers, I am sure you will find them as bizarre as anything you have ever read."

Val was equally certain that he was right in that assumption.

Tony then recounted some of the words he recalled. He prefaced it all by telling her that words were written like a teenager writing to his first girlfriend, but that he was drawn into every word on every page.

He quoted one bizarre reading he had finished reading the previous night.

"Hey, lady, if you are wondering who killed your man let me tell you, I did it. Yes, I did it for two good reasons. One, your man has been bad news for a lot of big shots in town. He sure got a lot of guys pissed at him. I guess he stepped on too many of the important people in town. They didn't like his sticking his nose into their business. I heard from many of them that he had been given more than a hint to stop poking his nose into things that were none of his business. I had my own reasons for wanting to get rid of him. I wanted him out of our world, so we could really get together. Each day I wake up and cry out, Annette. As I lie down in bed each night I shout out, Annette. It shouldn't come as a surprise to you about how much I feel about you. I love how you have been so kind and so nice to me."

Tony went on to tell her of the town bemoaning the loss of the good doctor but he did not understand the disregard which prevailed over most of the town in capturing the man or men who had caused this killing.

Valerie was intrigued by all she heard and she decided to be the one who found out what prompted this killing. She was totally puzzled as to who had the most to gain by this dreadful slaying. Was this murder committed due to the writer's need for Annette or was it purely a business deed.

Moments later she and Tim entered Tony's place. She was gratified when Tim looked around the cabin shouting

"It looks just like it always did."

Beaming at him, she passed him five pens and five paper sheets.

"Listen up, my friend. We are here to do some important work. I want you to write a message to Tony saying 'Come home soon Tony we need you here.'"

Tim's job was to very slowly copy those words on the five sheets and then pin each sheet around the entire room.

"Wow that is a great idea. It sure will shake up Tony when he gets home."

Valerie was pleased that her ploy had struck home. She added that Tim should see to it that each written word was legible. This trying task was assigned to Tim so that he should be totally occupied while Valerie was free to go through every inch in the cabin to see if there was anything of interest left there.

She scurried through the room intent on finding any hidden secrets but found nothing of value. Three times she opened and closed each and every drawer from end to end but found nothing of interest available.

Tim and Valerie could not have been more intense in their work on their appointed chores. Tim never got around to finishing more than one sheet before he saw Valerie waving a bed pillow case in the air and shrieking out "WHAT THE HELL IS THAT."

A much startled Tim nearly fell off the chair he sat on while doing his writing. She had frightened him beyond words. He shouted back to her.

"What the, what the, and then in an equally loud voice shouted back at her, WHAT THE HELL are you screaming about?"

Valerie had dropped the pillow and now was waving a single page in the air. She had lost all control, as she kept waving the page in the air. She sensed that she was reading the title page of the papers and its title was, 'THE WONDERS OF ANNETTE.'

She dug further into the pillow case and found some fifteen other sheets. They were obviously the writings that Tony had told her of. As she continued her perusal of the pages she started reading the words aloud. On the very first page the following was written.

"To all who will be reading the following pages, do know that I am as puzzled by them as you are. I write these first words so that all who read what will follow will know that this is not some piece of fiction but is reality at its worst."

She started reading aloud in the hope that the words would then be easier to comprehend.

Tim found it difficult to understand the meanings of the words Val sang out to him. Actually he did not comprehend much of what she said. He kept nodding as if this reading was meant just for him. His mouth remained ajar but no meaning came through to him.

As Val continued with her reading, Tim looked at her as if she was shouting meaningless syllables that had no meaning. He wished that Tony was doing the reading for he would explain every spoken word.

Valerie kept racing through the pages thinking that the answers were but a few pages away. She hurriedly read through the next page and then the next page and then read right through to the final page.

When she was finished she was as confused as Tim. She decided to read through all the pages once again.

She was even more at a loss when she had finished the second reading.

In his first talking of these pages, Tony told her that they would not be easily understood.

"These writing will be most troublesome to understand, but stick to them, and I am sure it will reveal the strangest of happenings."

Indeed, she found the remaining writings all but undecipherable. Each page left a strange and bewildering script that dazed her.

Tim was totally confused, and Valerie could do nothing to explain what she was reading. Any sense of meaning eluded her.

She could hardly decipher letter from letter but bit by bit the words seemed merge into a meaning that left her wondering. She read and then reread practically every paragraph, She was never certain if she really was understanding what she was reading, 'I sit here hating myself. Annette, what had begun as a silly fixation soon became an obsession that grew into a need I could not ignore? My love for you is behind the dreadful deed I did. My love for you swept away any sense of control that might have prevented me from taking my passion to the horrid end it pushed me. My entire life is on the edge of total collapse. I am about to leave beautiful Ashland in search of a world where I can start my life anew.

There is little doubt but that I will never forgive myself. I will never blame you, Annette, for the forthcoming consequences. Please believe me. Yes, I did it for you. You also should know that though it was I that pulled the trigger there were others who knew and approved of that shot being fired.

Please know that I regret what I have done. But, also know that I was driven by passion. It was passion for you that triumphed over every other thought. I beg your forgiveness, in this oh so strange writings.

Chapter Fifty-Three

Valerie was totally befuddled by the strange writings she was reading. The words told of a killing, yet the killer's name was never disclosed. Was there really a killing? Was the writer the killer and just who was he? Nothing in her limited knowledge of Ashland's history led to anything about a vicious murder.

Who was this woman Annette that he talks about?

If there was a killing, who was the man he killed? Did he do it of his own accord or were others involved as well?

Valerie could not find any notation about what had occurred on that very sad day. There was no signature on those lost words. Surely they were not written in Tony's handwriting. All she could determine was total puzzlement.

Her thoughts were slowly driving her mad. Who was the dead person and, more importantly, who was the killer? Who was Annette and what had she done to spur on the killing?

Valerie thought she was on to something yet the more she assumed the less she believed. Above all else she did not have a clue as to how she should proceed. Her head was abuzz with things she should do. But the most bothersome was her fear of what would happen if she spread the word of the killing.

First, she must get to Rich. No. First she must reread more of these strange words Tony had bequeathed to them. No. First thing she must do is to dry out this mess of papers. No. First she had to somehow find the date this had occurred.

No. No. No. No. First, she must stop crying.

Of course, she did none of the above. She hurriedly started to stuff all the newly found pages back into the still damp pillow case. Next she started out the front door only to be interrupted by Tim who quietly asked, "Valerie should I come with you, or should I just wait here?"

The question awoke the dazed young woman who rushed back to Tim, kissed his cheek as hard as she could and then dragged him out of the cabin.

As they stumbled down the hill, she recalled the words she had just read. It turned her very grey. She strongly believed that Tony had advised her of this gibberish because of his inability to make any sense of these pages. Finding out who had written these perplexing pages and what these words meant became her sole mission.

There was little doubt in her mind that the writer was telling a story that would lead its leaders down a path that would totally confuse them. Yet there was nothing in his confession that led one to who he was.

The words Tony had written pleaded for readers of the piece to believe in what he had written. Typical of Tony, his words offered up only the facts as he knew them. His last sentence pleaded that the entire piece may sound weird but despite that they must accept all that they read.

In his mind, one very young and idiotic soul had committed this dire crime. It had to be the same man who had written these words.

Hiding the papers in a garage wall was mad or did it ensure that one day the garage would yield up this horrid event to all of Ashland.

Tony's limited words ignited Val's thinking process. One reading, and she had all of his words memorized and, per se, was totally confused. Only one clue jumped from the remaining pages. It was the old fashioned writing that led her to the belief that they had been written many, many years ago. She had no doubts that the piece had been written and then hidden away well over one hundred year ago.

Undoubtedly, Tony must have been as confused by them as Valerie was. A wall had to be torn down and a mystery opened for him to try to decipher. Had he instantly understood what the words meant or was he as in doubt of them as she was?

After readings those confusing words for the first time, he thought that he had been purposely hired so as to reveal what was hidden in the wall. But knowing the man who had led him to these dire pages, Tony knew there was no room to cast guilty looks at the man. Surely that wall would have eventually fallen down of its own accord.

He was doing the job so as to earn a couple of bucks and nothing else. The sordid mystery that his work had revealed was a frightening shock to him. Inadvertently, he had stumbled upon a series of words that led to a tale of an unthinkable event. The complex words which filled his heart, mind, and soul – left him more than dumfounded by the story that poured forth.

At first, Tony felt that he should bring it to the Chief of Police. But he turned away from that idea for fear of what they might suspect him of. He was frightened of turning to others to help unravel this mystery that he faced. Could he be accused of some nefarious involvement with all of this? Had the original piece really been written recently and made to look as if the real villain was alive and well and looking for others to be accused of a hideous murder?

Tony thought it would be wise to add a disclaimer and place it first on page 1.

'My name is Anthony D'Angelo. I have lived most of my life in Ashland. I am the head of a team of men who tend to the Cemeteries of Ashland. We do a great job keeping those cemeteries quite presentable. What you are about to read definitely ties itself to earlier days when a horrendous crime was committed in this peaceful village.

The readings never revealed who was killed, nor why the crime was perpetrated. It had been written in the early 1900's. In said book many pages spoke of a horrid murder. The fact that the killer in this case was never found became a scandalous story that the city had to live with.

Tony was totally confused by the event and the papers that told of the event. There was no raison d'être offered for the killing. The words he had stumbled upon revealed nothing that could point to a killer. Yes, the writer of those words claimed to have been the killer, but nothing in his writings substantiated that fact.

Tony's writings offered only his oath that he in no way had anything to do with the killing. Instead he stressed that he was also uncertain that the writer of these pages was also the killer. What most bothered him was that he didn't have a single clue as to who the killer was.

Chapter Fifty-Four

$\mathcal{V}$alerie and Tim got home while their apartment was still sun lit. They were both anxious to get Rich involved in all this craziness. Tim repeatedly asking Valerie where Rich was and her answer that Rich and several other actors were still at the theatre working on a new play was not at all to his satisfaction.

"Why is Rich doing something dumb when I am so scared? You can't tell me anything. Tony isn't here and I need to talk to someone who can help me. I need Rich now."

He paused for a moment and seemed to be pondering the situation he faced.

Minutes passed as the frown on his face slowly lessened. Several times he turned to Valerie, but no words came forth from him. Finally, he managed to look straight at Valerie and, in a most quiet tone, he managed to offer up one sentence as he asked, "Is it a Shakespeare play?"

"No you silliness. All the Shakespeare plays were written hundreds of years ago."

"Well suppose they found a new play that no one knows who wrote it. Just like what you read to me today. Suppose someone found a new Shakespeare play. Wouldn't that be important and wouldn't Rich and his friends want to act in that play?"

"I guess you are right. So, let's wait for him to come home and tell us all about what they were doing today."

Tim was in one of his very rare bad moods. He wanted an answer and he wanted it now. He was bothered that Rich was not here when he was needed so much. Valerie was not to be questioned, so he merely turned away from her and went to hide under his bed.

He mumbled to himself that he wished Tony was here. Tony always gave him answers and then explained what it all meant. If Tony were here all of them would understand what all that writing was about.

By now he was in a real pout. He thought he would get out from under the bed and yell at Valerie but just then he heard her call out to him, "Timmy, do you want vanilla or chocolate ice cream for dessert?"

Tim thought for about two seconds and then crawled out from the bed and smilingly ran back to Valerie, as he shouted out "Chocolate, Chocolate."

He followed that up by asking Valerie why you have to eat the whole meal before you get to the dessert which is what you really want.

"Well if you really love the server of the dessert as much as you love the dessert, then there's a good chance you might get a taste of that dessert before dinner."

It took Tim no time to get the message as he practically jumped on Valerie and planted a happy kiss on each of her cheeks.

3

A large taste of the dessert was delivered with great joy by Valerie as she happily accepted that Tim was back to being the sweetest teenager in the world.

Rich's gift for good timing must have been at its most promising, for at that very moment he walked into the kitchen just as Tim was wiping the chocolate off his face.

"This looks like a happy crew. Tim, have you been flirting with my girlfriend again?"

With a twinkle in his eye, Tim stuck his tongue out as he added, "She is nicer to me than you are. Would you believe that today she had me working with her on a big mystery?"

Rich looked to Val but her body movements and dissuading facial expressions puzzled him.

"Hold off there you two. I smell something is being hidden from me. I need an answer and I need it now."

Not a word came forth from Tim or Valerie

"All right, I guess there is something terrible you won't tell me so I'll have to commit suicide. He groaned quite loudly, extended his hands, grabbed his throat and slowly fell to the floor as he started to choke himself.

Tim thought that this was a new game Rich was playing so he joined in by jumping on Rich and choking him as well. He was joined by Valerie who kept blowing sweet kisses into Rich's ears.

Rich managed to get out one sentence, "I need help. If you two will tell me about what you are hiding, I'll tell all about my wasting my time on the worst play I have ever had anything to do with."

That intrigued his two assailants enough so that they released their foe, but they still remained atop him.

He got his breath back and told them that the man who claimed to be the latest Shakespeare was a fraud.

"He handed us one overly long piece of garbage that I and five other complaisant actors suffered through for far too long. It was torture reading through it and therefore we will not discuss it any further."

At which point Tim shouted out, "Good. Then there is no reason for us to talk about that Shakespeare guy anymore. Let's eat."

It wasn't until Tim had long since gone to watch his favorite TV show that Valerie grabbed Rich and pulled him into the living room. She sat him down on the softest of chairs and then kneeled beneath him.

"I've got the most important thing to tell you, and I want to pour it all out before you ask even one word. Kiss me and then we can have a serious talk."

The serious talk lasted for over an hour as she related everything she had read from those strange pages that Tony had discovered. Rich did not interrupt her discourse for even a second. He sat totally bewildered by it all. Each sentence she uttered brought more and more confusion to Rich. When she ended her dissertation they both just stared at one another.

Rich was as puzzled by her words as he had been when she had first started her dissertation. Neither one could find anything worthwhile in what Tony had given her.

Valerie's reading excited them both but had left them totally puzzled by it all.

Chapter Fifty-Five

The following morning, Rich and Valerie were at the Ashland library studying a book which the head librarian had referred them to. The words were exciting, but they did not open up any new doors for them.

Valerie and Rich spent that entire morning reading aloud to one another. Both, all too quickly, became bored, what with their rapidly shouting out of names and statistics of the big wigs of those days.

Further studying of the book did reveal vast sections that spoke of activities which confirmed almost word for word what Tony written.

Of greatest value, was the detailed discussion of the business activities that kept the rich and the near rich involved in eternal battles to acquire greater and greater wealth. The dollars changing hands was pursued with ardent fervor. A great deal of the money came with the purchase and sale of land.

Some of the land was to be used for the ever-demanding need for new housing and commercial purposes. But it was the four letter word that really stirred excitement in the little town.

Gold, the product that had brought worldwide fame to California hit the Ashland area with much excitement. The California residents who dared to try Oregon as a new gold haven swiftly discovered it was not in the plenitude as California was. Yes, several promising strikes were made in the waters of Ashland but they were enormously undersized as compared to their southern counterparts. The lure of gold in Oregon was tempting but did not deliver close to what had gone on in the state south of them.

The simple little town of Ashland was brilliantly situated close to California. The mountains were beautiful, the promises of a great climate that yielded ease of living and, of course, the possibility of striking gold tempted many families and equal numbers of single men on the prowl for gold fortunes.

The book did dwell on a Doctor Rountree and his wife, Annette, who had excitedly moved to Ashland. Like others the excitement of future enrichment intrigued both the good doctor and his wife.

Their unique weapons in this battle was in much contrast to all the other new comers to Ashland. They never joined the fight to discover the gold lode that would be a winner for them. It was the battles waged between the wealthy of Ashland who fought over the constant money flow that brought forth what attracted them.

The wealthy of Ashland were noted for the fierce battles they waged with one another. Old friends became ardent enemies in the battle to be a winner in the gold race and even more so for who controlled the land.

Newcomers, like the doctor and his wife, were treated with disdain in the fight that led to greater wealth. Yet despite the open disregard they were shown by the current leaders of the town, the doctor and his beautiful wife, slowly but surely began to win more than their fair share of the battles.

Great animosity grew from the battles. Long term friends forgot what was more important, maintaining a friendship or claiming another yield of gold. Most failed at this never ending preoccupation with acquisitions. Being an enemy of a onetime friend triumphed over honoring a friend of days gone by.

The poor of the town were enthusiastic backers of Annette for her graciousness and her beauty. They had nothing but applause for the doctor who healed them of all illnesses. His fees for taking care of their needs were amazingly small and brought applause from all, yet his capability to match dollar for dollar with the wealthy of the town brought him nothing but scorn from the adversary group who had, singularly led all financial doings prior to his coming into town

What gave this odd couple their greatest joy was winning the many economic fracases that kept arising. Yes, the dollar return was important, but of greater meaning was the frown on the faces of the men they had just defeated.

Rich and Valerie were constantly shouting out at one another with a fact they had just picked out of the book or questioning if that was what Tony meant about some people in a certain paragraph he had written.

Tim understood nothing of the preoccupation with all sorts of people. To him only two people mattered and they lived in the same house as he did.

"You guys are sure nutty. First, you tell me that most of what you are reading is over one hundred years old. I wake up after a long nap, and you are still arguing about one hundred years ago. I don't understand one word of what you are saying, so I'm going to the bathroom. Call me when dinner is served."

Valerie turned to Rich and quietly uttered, "Once again Tim has proven who the smart one is in our family."

Chapter Fifty-Six

*I*t was early afternoon the next day that Valerie and Tim walked into the local police station. Valerie had tutored Tim to just drop off the papers that Tony had given them. Once having done so he was to tell the officer there that his brother Rich had given him this package and told him to drop it off. Tim was also to tell the man that his brother, Rich, was an actor at the Shakespeare Festival and with that he was to walk out to where Val awaited him.

She did this because she felt his ineptitude in this effort would shield both of them from further involvement.

Tim fulfilled all that he had been told to do. He dropped the package off in the hands of the first officer he saw and immediately turned and left the station house. He was halfway down the stairs leading from the police station when the same policeman he had delivered his package to came scrambling after him, while shouting "Hey you stop right there."

Valerie was carefully filing away on her fingernails until the shouting of the policeman got her attention. Rather angrily, she looked up at the policeman and shouted back up at him, "Please stop screaming at the boy. He won't understand you and he will get frightened by all the noise you are making."

She turned to Tim and said, "Don't worry about that silly man. He doesn't understand you and he has no reason to scream at you. Let's just leave him right now."

The policeman was rather bewildered by both the boy who merely kept walking away from him and the young woman who was berating him so. He stopped barking at the two of them and slowly turned back into the station house totally mystified by what had just transpired.

Valerie hurried Tim home, laid out his favorite meal and then dived into her bedroom or, as she called it, her writing room and disappeared for the afternoon.

It wasn't until late that evening when the three of them got back together and they could really relax. It had been a busy and tiring day. Tim quickly crawled into bed while Rich and Val held each other as they quietly watched the Colbert TV show. It was a pleasant way to ease off the pressures of each day.

Valerie closed her eyes and seemed ready to fall asleep when Rich nudged her.

"Hey, I forgot to tell you that Walt's secretary, Anne, told me that he wants to meet with us tomorrow morning. She didn't have a clue as to what he wanted to tell us, but she did say that he seemed very excited about the forthcoming meeting."

"That's odd. I can see him wanting to meet up with you but I can't imagine why he wanted to see me. What time is this meeting to happen?"

"She said any time between nine thirty and eleven would be fine. Look let's get there early and then have an early lunch."

"Okay, but let's skip the lunch which will let me get in some writing time. I'm deep into that book I've told you about, and I'm anxious to move the plot along. I am having so much fun with my new life that I wonder why I ever tried acting when writing is the real world I want to live in."

Rich just nodded his head as he pondered what could Walt want from them. Truth of the matter was that it led to a very sleepless night and a very early rising time for both of them.

Not a minute after nine-thirty, both of them stood outside Walt's office peering in at Anne who was deep into a phone conversation.

Both Val and Rich were somewhat annoyed as they impatiently waited for someone to acknowledge their presence. The phone call remained endless and Walt could well be in China for he certainly was not in the theatre.

Rich and Valerie took turns pacing up and down the halls that surrounded Walt's office. They hadn't eaten any breakfast that morning so as they would not be late for this meeting. Each of them began pacing up and down the hall awaiting Walt's s arrival but their patience was slowly beginning to turn to anger when Walt dashed into his office screaming at Anne to get her ass off the phone and with a wild swing of his arms invited the two pacers to join him inside his office.

Per usual his blond hair was uncombed and he kept running both hands through them almost in sync with every word he uttered.

"You know sometimes I think this job is only fit for a man with two heads."

He then shouted out to Anne that three coffees and several Danish were immediately needed. He ended that outburst by quietly asking how they were doing this glorious morning.

Chapter Fifty-Seven

Rich and Valerie didn't have a clue on how to respond to Walt. They stared at each other and then at Walt who just sat there with a smile growing larger by the moment as he stared back at them. Obviously, he was enjoying their puzzlement, as they just looked his way but said nothing.

Finally Val managed to get out an embarrassing "We are having a wonderful day today, aren't we?"

This brought forth a loud guffaw from Walt. He finally stopped laughing as he managed to get out the words, "Okay, I give in. I have something wonderful to tell you, but if you laugh at what I have to say I may have to beat you into saying I am brilliant."

He paused again as he offered up the coffee and edibles. He kept staring at each of them before finally accepting the fact that there would not be anything forthcoming from either one.

"Tell me something, when are you two getting married?"

Both exploded at the same moment but in different words saying "As soon as we can" from Valerie and "The day after the Festival closes down" from Rich.

Walt's rejoinder led to even greater confusion on the parts of Rich and Val.

"Great. That fits right into my plan. "

He let those words sink in and then offered up "I'm sure both of you have heard that this next season we will be presenting a Shakespeare play that we haven't done in over fifteen years."

Not being privy to any of the forthcoming shows that could be presented in the coming season, they merely gaped at Walt who, in turn, did not give them so much as a hint about the title of said show and just quietly waited for some sort of response. The two faces staring at him offered nothing new to the conversation.

Walt finally told them that it was one of his most favorite of all the plays that Shakespeare had ever written.

"When we decided to produce this show I laid claim to being its director, and I want you two to take the title roles."

Rich and Valerie were stunned and voiceless. First of all they were shocked he had not told them the name of the play and, secondly, with Val's current dilemma about being an actress or a writer they could not find any words with which to respond. Two blank faces just stared out at him.

"Nothing, huh?"

Rich and Val sat there wondering where it was going and how all this would involve them.

By now Walt was up and walking around mentally kicking around the words that would best describe what he had in mind.

"If I am correct, I think I've added another aspect to the shows that will bring in hordes of ticket purchasers and will add another dimension to the play."

He looked to them for a reply but none was forthcoming. They blankly stared at him while wondering what the hell he was talking about.

"My idea depends on a deal I have to make with you two. First off, I am giving you the Bowmer Theatre, absolutely free of charge, to serve as to where your wedding will be performed. Is that agreeable to you?"

Rich almost jumped out of his skin with a smile that was the largest one that had ever graced his face. Val nearly pushed Walt out of his chair, as she dashed to him grabbed his face with both her hands and implanted a kiss that seemed beyond stopping.

They uttered no words, but beamed their delighted approval of Walt's plan.

Walt rose from his chair as he waved a pointed finger at the two. "Now just one moment. You haven't heard what I want from you. You have to pay for my treating you to the Bowmer. I came up with this idea one day when I watched the two of you just holding hands and staring at one another. It was beautiful to see."

Valerie was the first to react with a stuttering "But you know that I may be giving up acting."

"Nonsense, this is the first chance you've ever had to really challenge yourself. I want two people who totally love one another getting at each other, and I mean on and off the stage. It should produce incredible stage sparks."

Rich was with Walt immediately but said nothing so that the decision was all Val's. She was completely confused as to whether she wanted it or that she hated Walt for tempting her so.

"You two are ideal for the roles. Yes, I am bribing you to take the parts. It's a no-lose shot for you. You'll both be on fire from the first reading we do, and it will grow in depth and fun with each subsequent reading. Now get your asses out of this office. Your scripts will be on Anne's desk until five o'clock this afternoon. If it is still there when I come in tomorrow, I will still love you but the deal will be off. Oh yes, the play's title is **'Romeo and Juliet.'**

Chapter Fifty-Eight

$\mathcal{R}$ich and Val walked ever so slowly down the street. Neither of them spoke a word. They reached their apartment where they were greeted by Tim who suggested, "Boy, you two look like shit."

Normally, this would have gotten at least a rebuke from Rich, but this day it didn't even draw a frown. Today found both of them staring at the package that Rich had thrown on the table.

Val slowly picked up her carving knife and was now pointing it at the chicken she had just taken from the fridge. But she didn't cut one piece of meat that now lay on the table looking up at her.

In her effort to prepare lunch for the three of them, she again held the knife she had dropped on the kitchen counter. The knife remained poised over the chicken, but their sandwiches remained sans chicken.

Rich sought refuge in the bathroom. Without opening his fly or dropping his pants he sat down on the toilet seat.

He kept reaching for the toilet paper but only to twirl the rolls of paper around and around and around.

He awoke to what he was doing when he heard Tim shouting out to him, "Hey Rich, are you stuck in there?"

Rich quickly emerged, as Valerie was yet again pondering why the chickens remained breadless.

It was Tim who awakened the two of them.

"Hey, when did the two of you die? I'm hungry so will one of you make my lunch?"

He had uttered the proper words which seemed to spur Valerie into action, as she very slowly started preparing sandwiches and as Rich poured out three glasses of milk.

They avoided looking at one another until all had eaten all they could.

"Hey do you guys mind if I eat the rest of the sandwiches you both have left on your plates?"

Without a word, both slid their plates over to Tim who quickly devoured them. He thanked them with his mouth full of their lunch.

Valerie walked from the table and then turned back to Rich.

"Well, what do you think?"

"I haven't come up with a single thought. If I forced you to do something that was all about what I want, that would be unfair to you and I couldn't do that. This has to be a joint decision."

"And, I can't make up my mind because I know you are dying to play Romeo."

Tim, speaking with a mouthful of food shouted out, "You two are bugging me. What the heck are you talking about?"

Both Rich and Valerie broke out into laughter. It was Val who first ceased laughing as she asked, "Tim, would you answer me if I asked you a very serious question?"

Rich jumped in saying that the question was simple enough. "We have a chance to have our wedding in the Bowmer Theatre. Should we agree to have it there or not?"

Tim pondered the question for quite a while before answering, "Will we still get to clean up the bathrooms after you get married?"

"I think I can assure that."

"Well then do it. But you have to wait until Tony gets back so he can be at the wedding."

Rich took but one glance as Val announced, "Once again we learn from the young one. Val I think the decision has been made for us. Do you agree with me?"

"Without a question. But first I must make our wise one a thank you sandwich."

The last sandwich was done in minutes and eaten seconds later. Val and Rich started out the door. Halfway out Rich spun around and spun back to grab Tim off with them.

Fifteen minutes later, they walked through the offices of the Shakespeare Festival and headed to Walt's office.

Anne looked up as the entourage approached her desk. She picked up one of the package that lay on her desk and smilingly handed it to Rich.

'What took you so long? And is this the Tim who is the famed cleaner of our bathrooms."

"Yes, I'm that Tim. Did you know that Rich and Val are getting married and they are going to be my Father and Mother? It was Val's idea that I go with them when they go off on their honeymoon. I don't know what that means, but Val said we would have a lot of fun on it. What's your name?"

"My name is Anne, and I am sure you will have a great time on your honeymoon."

Tim was about to launch into one of his great speeches when Rich took his arm and led him out of the room.

Chapter Fifty-Nine

wo weeks later, a very brief wedding ceremony was held in the jam-packed Bowmer Theatre. It was standing room only for the attendees at this most unusual wedding event.

Tim had never been so finely attired, but he refused to wear anything but his finest sneakers. Val had taken him to a men's wear shop and outfitted him from head to toe but Tim rejected wearing those heavy looking shoes. She also had the good sense not to fight off his rationale for the sneakers he would be wearing for the big event.

"I'm going to dance all night at the great party we will be having. I'll need my favorite sneakers to keep me dancing as much I'm going to do. Since I will be the best man for the wedding, I must also be the best dancer."

It was a statement of fact that no one dared dispute.

The many 'hams' attending the ceremony being staged before them were quiet and respectful. All paid homage to this unique wedding and the place it was being staged in.

However, when the Mayor of Ashland, a friend of Walt's, very solemnly offered, "I now pronounce you man and wife," Tim screamed out at the loudest he could ,"Hallelujah" which brought forth cheering from everyone at the wedding and an enormous smile from Tim.

When questioned about why he had offered his outburst, he smilingly replied, "I was afraid something might go wrong, and they wouldn't be married and I wouldn't ever have parents."

His little speech reached out to far more of the wedding crowd than the wedding couple did. As he neared the end of this mass of people Tim almost knocked over Walt who he had met earlier that evening. With joy, he kissed Walt and then kept hugging and kissing every one he passed be they male or female.

Rich and Valerie scooted out of the theatre with cheers covering their every step. Tim knew only his fellow bathroom cleaners, but not knowing someone, did not stop him from shouting out. "Hey, did you know those two are my new parents."

He beat a path towards Lithia Park where he caught up with the newlyweds and where a dozen fine musicians were tuning up, as table after table were being filled with plates loaded with every type of food one could desire.

The park was soon filled with all of the wedding participants as well as dozens of young people who raced in from the square around the corner where they spent most days and nights.

They too joined in with what promised to be a joyous time. They brought with them many, many guitars and a joie de vive that delighted all. The greeters included the professional musicians who had been hired for this gala event. Soon the music had people dancing on the grass and singing along as loud as they could.

Rich and Val stood on a little knoll observing the wild party that was spread before them. He clung fiercely to Val, while letting Tim go back and forth welcoming all the attendants to this very great party.

The newlyweds were delighted with the madness erupting all around them. At one point Tim rushed up to his newly named parents and shouting out as loud as he could, "Aren't we the luckiest people in the world."

Val pulled him to her and softly whispered in his ear "Our first child is the smartest boy in all of Ashland."

Chapter Sixty

$\mathcal{R}$ich knew almost every nook and cranny in New York City while Tim recalled a street or two, but to Valerie it was an adventure in a new world.

Rich became their personal guide while Val and Tim readily adjusted to being the usual New York tourists. Of course, each day included seeing plays and visiting Rich's old friends. The three agreed that someday they would be sharing more permanent time in this wonderful city, but for now all agreed that as much as they enjoyed New York, their immediate future would remain in Ashland.

Much as they tried to save money they could not escape the attraction of the delightful and expensive eating places. Rich did manage to take them to several very good but inexpensive restaurants. Truth be told, Val and Tim could not distinguish which was a more modest spot or a more expensive salon. This too produced yet another great Tim quote.

"You know some of these restaurants are almost as good as the ones in Ashland."

Yes, they had indulged themselves by spending their first night in town at a rather nice and rather expensive hotel. Rich did save them some money, as he managed to free load the three of them in one friend's home after another. Hotels were far too expensive to be indulged in. Granted, this meant taking at least one friend out to dinner each night.

Rich and Valerie had shared the daily costs but their dreamlike days soon came to an abrupt end. They were up early on the eighth day when Valerie advised Rich that her bank account in Ashland was very close to reaching the zero mark. The threesome packed their gear that night and bid New York a very fond farewell.

Chapter Sixty-One

Two weeks later, a very nervous group of people gathered around a large circular table in the Shakespeare Festival's rehearsal hall.

All were speechless and quite nervous while pretending to be at ease as they awaited the appearance of Walt. Every now and then an obviously phony laugh burst forth, which was quickly cut short by the person sitting nearest the laugher.

The actors had grouped together while trying to remain as cool as feasible. Though all were quite experienced in this ritual of learning all about what they would soon be presenting, they couldn't hide their nervousness from anyone.

This cast of over twenty actors were each holding a script of the famed '**Romeo and Juliet.**' Everyone present had spent the previous evening carefully studying their role, whether it be large or small. None had been more avid in this studying than Val and Rich. Despite the tension of the moment, most were secure in the knowledge that they would be great in the parts assigned to them. Others quietly hid their insecurity.

This was a significantly large ensemble of fine actors and their past experiences assured one and all that their 'Romeo' was sure to be a big hit.

The stage manager was busy in a deep discussion with his two assistants, as they discussed the nuances of how one character would relate to the other.

The set designer and his construction manager had previously met with Walt and felt assured that they were on the correct path to delivering the perfect set for this new production of this famed theatre piece. They were quietly whispering away while shifting their attention from one part of the stage to another. From these discussions, a delightful set would soon appear.

Several costume designers were into heavy discussions on colors and fabrics. The three choreographers were locked into heavy thoughts of movement, while the fight director, a sound designer, a dramaturge, an assistant director, two light designers, and a voice and text coach were busy quietly assessing what their role would be in the complex staging of this show.

All seated had one objective in mind. This show would be yet another smash hit for the Ashland Shakespeare Festival.

The only folk who were truly at ease were the two music composers, who had already written over fifteen pieces that they knew would add moments of delight to the ears of every audience member.

Despite the crowd, little noise emanated from this ever ready group. Each of them had been involved in play after play both in Ashland and for theaters throughout the country. Despite their renowned expertise a special tension worked its way through each of them. Yet, one sensed that each of this group were more than confident about what lay ahead for them.

It was expected that the actors would be nervous on this first day. Several of them had already spent a good deal of time in studying their parts. Some had even started memorizing bits of their roles. But today would be devoted to determining what Shakespeare meant by those brilliant sentences he had put together in bringing out the unique story.

The one missing ingredient was that the director of this piece had not made his appearance as yet. Twenty minutes flew by before Walt strode in to be greeted with a ton of cheers that was more a signal that all were anxious to get to work than a greeting to Walt.

Ever the salesman, he greeted almost everyone present. A kiss here, a warm hand shaken here and there, and he was soon up on the stage. He was warming up every member of his team as he looked out on this mob of people seated in front and around him. It took him several moments before he shouted out, "Thank you Mr. Shakespeare."

All tension seemed to immediately disappear.

Walt waved his script at the actors gathered beneath him and this brought forth further cheers.

"Yes, I'm as excited to be directing this unusual piece of genius as all of you are about appearing in it. I know we are going to do justice to this epochal play. Let me guarantee you that your work will be beautiful, exciting, hilarious, and as gratifying as any show you have ever worked on."

He paused, looked to all in the theatre and very softly said, "Let's get to work."

Walt set them off by pointing directly at the lead dramaturge as he advised one and all, "That woman sitting there so silently amongst us is, as you know, our lead dramaturge. She advised me that what we are about to tackle is a breeze since Shakespeare only utilized One Hundred and Twenty Five Thousand words in creating this piece. I'll leave it to you to consider whether or not she knows what she is talking about."

To which the dramaturge loudly shouted back "Let's start with the talented assemblage we put together and see what we do with these long acclaimed words."

Chapter Sixty-Two

Four hours later, Rich and Valerie stumbled into their rather tiny apartment. They were more than spent. Having lead roles led to everyone in the theatre listening intently to each word they had uttered. The pressure of merely speaking those famed words was not done casually.

It seemed as if those two roles were the only ones that mattered. Each word they spoke drew serious attention from all in the theatre. At this point in the rehearsal, their job was to merely speak the words Shakespeare had written, but they knew that every word they uttered was being keenly listened to.

Their speeches led to questions from Walt and others seated in the theatre. Of greatest importance was that everyone understood every thought being presented.

Almost every line read aloud drew important attention and much discussion. Should one of those listening to the presentation be confused or wondering about the true meaning of what was spoken, a deep discussion could emerge as to exactly what said lines meant. Clarity of meaning was of greatest import.

All there knew that every sentence of Shakespeare's verbiage must emerge crystal clear and not leave any doubt as to their meaning.

For Valerie and Rich, or should we say Romeo and Juliet, the mere reading of their lines was more than exhausting for both of them.

That night, like all the others to come, Val and Rich slugged down a stiff shot of Scotch as soon as they arrived home and then pulled out their scripts play.

Rich cleared his throat and then harrumphed several times before reaching out and reading Romeo's first speech to Juliet.

Romeo
If I profane with my unworthiest hand this holy shrine, the gentle fine is this, – My lips, two blushing pilgrims, ready to smooth that rough touch with a tender kiss.

Juliet
Good pilgrim, you do wrong your hand too much, Which mannerly devotion shows in this, For Saints have hands that pilgrims do touch, and palm to palm is holy palmers do touch. And palm to palm is holy palmers' kiss.

Romeo
Have not Saints lips, and holy palmers too?

Juliet
Ay, pilgrim, lips that they must use in prayer.

Romeo
O, then, dear saint, let lips do what hands do. They pray;
grant thou; lest faith turns to despair.

Juliet
Saints do not move, though grant for prayers sake.

Romeo
Then move not, while my prayer's effects I take. Thus from
my lips, by yours, my sin is purged.

Rich interrupted their rehearsal as he gave Val a great big kiss and said, "This is the part of Romeo and Juliet that I like best."

At this point, Tim interrupted their work with a single sentence.

"What language are you speaking in?"

"Tim, you amaze me. We are speaking English."

Val jumped in saying that what Rich meant to say is that they were speaking old fashioned English which is what all folks spoke when Shakespeare, the author of this piece, wrote all his wonderful plays.

"Well, I don't care how good he writes his plays. For sure if I can't understand what he says I won't like his plays."

Rich again jumped in.

"Okay. Let me give you another speech that Romeo gives to the Nurse after Juliet has left the stage."

With that Rich reopened his script and turned to the following passage.

"Oh, she doth teach the torches to burn bright! Her
beauty hangs upon the cheek of night like a rich jewel in an

Ethiop's ear, Beauty too rich for use, for earth too dear! So shows a snowy dove trooping with crows, as yonder lady oe'r her fellow shows. The measure done, I'll watch her place of stand, and, touching hers, make blessed my rude hand. Did my heart love til now? Forswear it, sight! For I ne'er saw true beauty til this night."

"I think I would rather go to a baseball game than listen to that junk."

Val looked at Rich. He in turn extended his arm to her. "Script, Please."

She duteously handed same over.

"Tim, you are the wisest man I know so, accordingly, Val and I are closing these pages. Since there is no baseball game being played in town this evening, we are going to whatever restaurant you fancy."

Tim smiled at Rich and Val while saying, "Now that's a language I understand."

And thus their days and nights seemed to fly away. Rehearsals became more serious and much more strenuous. Tim adapted to Rich and Val going at one another in that funny language during their evening sessions. Fact of the matter was that he made a game out of their verbiage by trying to understand what was said. Yes, he sometimes began to grasp a sentence or two but nothing of consequence came through to him. A triumph was the rare moments when he understood a complete sequence.

"You know something, Rich, I think I'm beginning to understand everything Val says but I'm far from knowing what you are trying to say. It just seems like you are very mean to her, and I don't like that."

It was Val who was the first to grab Tim and heartedly squeeze him. "You know, Tim, I think I would rather marry you than your silly brother."

Rich stared blankly from Tim to Val. He slowly began to realize that Tim's criticism was spot on. Shakespeare had bestowed words to Romeo and Juliet which left their true feelings about the other rather obscure. Of course, both were quite interested in the other but their early words depicted disinterest.

Both Rich and Val stared at one another and then began to laugh rather heartedly. Rich quickly grabbed his jacket and then threw another one to Val and Tim. Within seconds, they were all out the door.

Chapter Sixty-Three

The weeks that followed intensified pressure on everyone involved in this so important production. Each discussion grew louder as passages began to be viewed differently on the how and why of certain passages. The most common gripe was, "Well, it is Shakespeare so what else would you expect?"

Even Walt was discrete about his criticisms, making them sound more like questions about what Shakespeare really meant in certain passages.

At the end of the second week, Walt rose and thanked them all for what they had endured during the past days and then added what he knew they were expecting that these easy days would soon be over.

"We'll start at ten o'clock Monday morning, and I'll expect you to go at it without scripts in hand. So have fun this weekend doing nothing but memorizing every word in your role. Kisses to you for these two weeks. Personally, I will get very drunk so that I can ready myself for the anger you will express to me come Monday morning. But just listen to what I have to say about this production. It is going to be a smash hit thanks to your great talents."

Hugs and kisses became the common activity as they all headed out of the Rehearsal Hall. They did so knowing that come Monday, they would be rehearsing in the Bowmer. Reality would be setting in with all its fierceness.

It was Valerie who stopped a bunch of the younger folk involved in this epic production with a quietly spoken sentence.

"Hey, why don't you all hop over to our house, and we'll eat and drink up a storm in honor of our last days of freedom before Mister Shakespeare devours us all."

To say the least her suggestion was heartily accepted by one and all. Within the hour their small apartment was filled with a noisy crew of theatre people who were busily eating and drinking and screaming at one another.

Tim just stood by watching all those crazy people slowly getting liquored up. He tried to join the party but the only drink he could handle was a full glass of Pepsi, so he quietly went off to his bedroom and fell asleep watching TV.

Val and Rich were great hosts and managed to have at least two to three drinks with each of their guests. They did little eating as the number of people eating soon devoured all that was edible in the house. With the next few hours, the crowd began to dwindle down, and soon Rich and Val found themselves alone and as drunk as could be.

Hugging her as hard as he could he whispered in her ear, "I have a rather strong desire to do to you what Romeo wants to do to Juliet?"

"Oddly enough I do believe that ere long Juliet will be much in favor of joining in with Romeo in doing exactly what he was referring to."

"Tell you what Juliet, why don't we hop into the bedroom and rehearse that scene in there."

Within moments they had stripped down and embarked on the wildest and most enjoyable scene they could imagine. Ten crazy minutes on the bed led to two naked people lying atop one another while laughing crazily away. It took many minutes for them to collapse and disappear into a dead sleep.

They awoke late the next morning totally hung over with the voice of Tim shouting out "Hey, I'm hungry. How about getting up and making me breakfast, and while you're doing that, how about putting on some clothes. You look ugly with everything you have sticking out."

His umbrage to them did little to improve their current sense of reality. Each, groaningly raised their heads and glared at Tim.

Val turned her head towards Rich. It was not a pleasant sight. She then turned towards the mirror which was on the bedroom closet. At first she thought who is that slut in our room? Then she realized that she was the slut in the mirror. It brought up thoughts of committing suicide.

Rich had already had enough of a look at Val and himself and had been mortified by what he had seen. The blanket he was lying upon was soon covering Val and his bathrobe was pulled up from the floor and covered every naked inch of his body.

"Val, I don't think I have ever been so drunk in all my life. Do you recall anything from last night?"

"The last I remember is standing on a kitchen chair and reciting Lincoln's Gettysburg Address."

"And I remember cheering you on for the great speech you were delivering."

"Rich, I really hate asking this next question, but did we have some wild sex last night?"

"Are you crazy? I don't remember anything but my trying to do a strip tease for everyone in the house, but I just kept falling on the floor."

"I also seem to recall you picking me up and throwing me over your shoulder and taking me somewhere or other."

"I don't remember anything like that. In fact I don't remember how I got into the bedroom, and I sure as hell don't remember how we got naked on our bed."

"Do you think Tim could remember anything about what we did last night?"

"Tim was in bed fast asleep within minutes of our coming home. He never likes crazy parties when he is uncertain about who most of the people are. I'm sure he was fast asleep long before we were."

"Well, I never want you and me to ever wake up again like we just did. Tim will forget this whole scene, but I will hate myself for what just transpired."

Rich and Val cowered in their wrappings. Val, very shamefacedly slipped into their bathroom while Rich buried himself under his bathrobe.

They shared one feeling. Each loathed themselves for whatever vile acts they must have performed the previous evening.

Chapter Sixty-Four

The intensity of rehearsals grew with each day, but as that grew, so did the confidence of each performer. All knew that a really fine performance was but days away.

Walt was so certain of this that, occasionally, he would disappear from a rehearsal confident that all would go well without him. He would appear for a few moments and then turn to all and announce that this was their time to resolve sections of the play that seemed to be puzzling them.

"Are you going to allow Mr. Shakespeare to stump us? I have total belief in your coming up with the answer to any of the little problems we have. I'll be back in an hour or two, and I'll be delighted with how you've resolved whatever is bothering you. Have fun and don't hurt one another."

And with that quip, he was off to help in another area of this very busy theatre company. They still had two weeks before opening night, so no one felt any pressure about his leaving them on their own.

It was just about then that Val began to feel extra tired after a particularly strenuous rehearsal. The excitement with the soon to arrive opening night added to the nervous apprehension about getting too tired to perform as well as she could. What seemed to bother her most was that her lifelong practice of exercising had all but disappeared. All she could think of was that no matter how hard she tried, her endless energy seemed to have disappeared.

She never mentioned this to anyone. Since no one queried her about her lack of energy she remained quiescent about it. No one, not even Rich, was aware of the travail Val was going through. Rehearsals were going well, and she felt totally at ease with how her Juliet was growing almost every day. Fact of the matter was that she was drawing a great deal of praise from company member after company member about how wonderfully her Juliet was growing.

Tim was the only one she knew who verbalized about her ever growing weariness. He and Val had often gone on slow runs up the neighboring hills but they had all but stopped.

"Hey, Val, if you don't take me on more trips up this mountain I'm going to get very fat."

That would prompt a short run up a hill, but she limited those adventures for her so busy life as an actress, a wife and Tim's quasi mother.

Two weeks later, the big day arrived. Opening night brought with it excitement, trepidation, hysterical fear of failure, assurance of success and, above all, thankfulness that all of their hard work had paid off. Their 'Romeo and Juliet' was going to be a roaring success.

The revues promised that this 'Romeo and Juliet' was one of the best ever presented. The stars were raved about' and ticket sales soared.

The first month was performed to sold-out houses and raves about the show. The only problem was Val's ever increasing weariness which had become more apparent to many in the company. Doing an afternoon matinee and then the evening's show was most taxing for her.

She very quietly told Rich that she was just exhausted after each performance. Each night she was fast asleep within an hour of getting home. Finally her despair drew her to a visit with the Dr. Edward Schiff who was long renowned as the finest physician in all of Ashland. He was a man famed for two things. The first was his sense of humor and the second his reputation as never being wrong in his analysis of what was ailing each of his patients.

From the first, he spent much time dryly querying her about the show. It seemed like he was more interested with her theatrical activities than her overall health.

"There is nothing wrong with you, Valerie. The only thing that I can tell you is something that is great news, and I am certain you already know about that. You are a very healthy lady for a pregnant young woman."

"I am what," came out very weakly from Val."

A very puzzled doctor explained that he was amazed that she was unaware of her status.

"From what you have told me and what I have determined I am certain that you are pregnant. I'll give you a month or two to continue dazzling all of us as Juliet and then you will triumphantly retire to a more important job. You will be delivering a wonderful child in about seven months. Congrats."

Somehow, Val found her way out of the doctor's office. As she stumbled down the street to her home the people facing her were perplexed by this very attractive woman who was obviously totally unaware of their presence. In turn they could not decipher any of what she was spitting out in an overly steady stream. Actually those words were quite simple.

"How could I be pregnant and my not know it? Rich always uses a condom. I remember my laughing at him when he has to get the damned thing off. He would get so mad at my mocking his dilemma with the damned thing."

She kept repeating the 'How' over and over, until she recalled the crazy party she and Rich had some months back. She stopped dead in her tracks' thus stranding herself in the middle of crossing a very busy thoroughfare. Cars began blasting their horns at Val who was oblivious to all.

She just stood there screaming out as loud as she could.

"Oh, yes, there I was opening my big mouth to the whole world to come to our house and get loaded. God knows what Rich and I did in that drunken state we were in at the end of that mad affair. Oh you drunken slut' thank you for getting yourself pregnant and goodbye to Juliet."

The cars began to circle around Val, with its drivers cursing at this nut case who seemed frozen in the middle of the street.

Somehow, she survived her stupidity and rushed home to Rich. The news she laid on him about her pregnancy stopped him dead in his shoes. He awakened with a grand hurrah then rushed to her and lifted her high over his head as he shouted out to her, "Did I hear you right? Are you really pregnant?"

Tim, totally confused asked out, "Will someone tell me what is happening and what that word means."

"It means pretty soon you'll have a little baby brother or baby sister to play with. Lucky ladies like Val get pregnant which means she is carrying a wonderful baby which is growing bigger and healthier each day,"

"Val, you and Rich confuse me. Whatever it is that Val has do we have to go to a store to buy one of those things, or do we have to write to some place and tell them ship one to us?"

Chapter Sixty-Five

The very next morning Val and Rich arrived at Walt's office long before even Anne was at her desk. This allowed them more time to prepare the correct words to offer up to Walt about how long Val would be playing the role she adored. Walt had told her time and time again that she was the perfect Juliet and he was more than proud of her. Indeed, Val was playing that role to perfection, and she loved the doing of it.

Both Val and Rich knew that, within a month or two, she could hardly present herself as that slim and lovely Juliet. No, no, the real Juliet was svelte and beautiful, while the word chubby was not acceptable when chatting about Juliet.

Rich of course was more than proud of his mother to be. Yes she would have to walk away from the role of her lifetime, but soon she would be the mother par excellence.

Walt, of course, rose to the occasion asking how long did she think she would look the part she was playing and, more importantly, how long she would want to play Juliet.

"My doctor gives me about a month or two before my Juliet would not be looking the part but, and I can't believe I am going to say this, but I would like to limit my time as Juliet to just what he suggests."

"Fair enough, my sweet Juliet, and would you be willing to work with your replacement while she learns how to perform the role? I can't think of anyone who would be better suited to do just that."

With that Val, embraced Walt, while saying out, "I was praying that you'd say that. Yes sir, I would love doing that."

"Well then come back in an hour and I'll introduce you to your replacement."

What she didn't reveal to anyone was that she was delighted with dropping her role as Juliet. She had proven that she could play that role as well as anyone. She was more than pleased that soon she would be a mother which thrilled her. But her favorite secret was that being fat was not a deterrent to being a writer, which was what she knew she would devote herself to.

Each day she thanked everyone who surrounded her. There could not be a better husband than Rich while Tim, as usual, was a delight to please. As a creative being her writing was a challenge to her which always made her happy. The need to create something new, something different, and most importantly, something that would excite the entire world was an amazingly motivating force.

Yes, being an actress had been a delight but the challenge of being a writer thrilled her to every core of her body.

The next thirty days seemed to fly by. First of all she was determined that everyone in the company would always think of her Juliet as the personification of how a

Juliet should be played. Yes, her replacement would most certainly deliver a bravo performance, but deep down Val knew that her enactment of that part was far better than anyone else could have delivered.

Throughout the month, she prepped herself to accept the fact that soon she would no longer be an actress but just another young mother. She had two valiant backers in this battle. Rich was the best of husbands while Tim, instinctively, rallied to her every need. Their constant support of her simply meant everything to her.

As the prime supporter in this battle, Rich was the perfect husband. He knew of the pressures his wondrous wife was enduring and made certain that he backed her totally in everything she thought of and did. Being an actor himself, he knew of the pain she must be suffering by having to give up a role she dreamed of performing.

Tim, on the other hand, could not understand why Val seemed to be home more and more of the time. Yet, loving her as much as he did, Tim accepted anything she did. His response to all the craziness floating around the house was simple enough. Bit by bit, he began to realize that he benefitted most with having her home. He sure liked that.

"I don't know what you are always talking about, but when we get that child, can it sleep in my room with me?"

Chapter Sixty-Six

After another month of being the starring actress in the lead role of Shakespeare's 'Romeo and Juliet,' Val was growing more and more physically exhausted. Since she was known for her strength, she decided it was time to see Dr. Schiff for the third time.

As soon as she entered Dr. Schiff's office, he greeted her with an even greater smile than normally. He had previously done extensive examinations on her which pleased him. The great smile on his face was even broader than usual. He grasped both her hands.

"Well, I've got some more great news for you today. There is no doubt in my mind, but that you will not be delivering one baby this year. You are going to bring two healthy and beautiful children into this world of ours."

With her mouth rather agape, Val managed to get out the words "Could you very slowly repeat what you just said?"

"What I just said is that I have for some time felt that you were going to deliver twins, and I now have all the conclusive evidence I need. The Ultra Sound Tests I have given you are shouting out the good news that you are carrying two beautiful babies in your tummy."

He smiled at Val waiting for her response to the wonderful news, but she just stared at him and offered nothing in return.

"Hey, I've just given you some great news. You are as healthy as can be, so your pregnancy and then your delivery should be as smooth as possible. Yes, this news might have shaken you a bit but, I assure you it means great days ahead for both you and your husband. I presume you or your husband have a twin brother or sister."

"No, there are no twins in either family."

"That's strange, but it just means that you and your husband are just plain lucky. I suggest that you scurry through your family history for the possibility that there is some history of multiple birth there. Normally, one or the other parent has some evidence of twin births in their family. But, whether there is or isn't, I assure you that you are the perfect mother to deliver twins. Your babies will be strong and beautiful. Just keep on with what you have been doing.

The two stood quietly facing one another, but it was Val who spoke first.

"You know I found you to be the perfect doctor for me. Today, for the second time, you have taken my breath away. But right now I know you are right and my husband will handle this with great joy. I'll bring him with me for my next exam. You and he will enjoy making fun of me, and our babies will come out smiling."

With that she kissed him on his forehead. She then stood up as tall as she could and pushed her belly out as far as it could go. As she reached the office door, she turned and flashed a huge flirtatious smile at him. It was her way of saying that all was well with her and his baby predictions were right on target.

Chapter Sixty-Seven

The months dragged by as Val grew bigger and bigger and as she grew, so did the smiles which claimed possession of her face. Yes, at times strange battles occupied various parts of her body. The smiles would disappear as pains would gather together and then attack different parts of her anatomy.

Some days would fly by with not one of her enemies attacking Val at all. Rich had made her swear to tell him when she was attacked by the bad guys, but it was rarely when she obeyed that edict.

Being just twenty-four and in fine condition, she handled the attacks on her body with some degree of platitude. She never let on to Rich when her major enemies attacked her simultaneously.

Fatigue, hemorrhoids, and heartburn were her main assailants. They were ruthless in the almost constant warfare against her but she found that singing the latest hit songs, somehow or other, managed to ease her most severe pain.

Unknowingly, Tim drove her almost insane when he kept telling her that her voice was like a sick hog pleading for release from jail. He suggested that she go for a walk whenever she felt the need to sing.

Strangely enough, Val found that Tim's advice did indeed help her. Because of him her walking increased almost double fold. She would return home, but with a smile on her face, and the pains greatly eased.

Rich was always coming home with some new pieces of gossip that was circulating through the company. When there was no succulent piece for her to delight over, he would come home with a new book to read or a special box of candy for her to devour. The candy might have added to her increasing weight problem, but it gave her hours of mental joy.

Tim seemed to be aglow and a bit confused by the laughter that constantly filled the apartment. He didn't have a clue as to what brought forth the laughter, but since it always put a smile on Val's face, he would laugh along with her.

His constant bit of advice to Val's most popular visitors was frequently delivered quite seriously.

"Ever since Val decided to stay home all the time, I have never been alone and that makes me happy as can be. You ought to come by here more often, and you will be happy too."

Tim was greatly puzzled by Val's almost daily growth. Each day she seemed to grow larger and larger, yet that growth didn't seem to bother her one bit.

He knew it was important to take care of Val, so early

in the game he began to watch over everything she did. At one point he decided that she spent too much time over her computer so he tried to dissuade her from poking away at it.

"You know if you did a little more exercise every day and less time at that machine of yours, you wouldn't be gaining weight and you would stop getting to look like a big fat cow."

Of course, there was no way to get her to do so.

"Tim, I love every minute I spend doing my writing. One of these days, people all over the world will be reading what I am writing now – at least I hope so."

Rich knew that his constant support of whatever she wanted to do was the best way to keep her happy. He kept laughing at her pains when they were at their worst. He mortified her and twisted her brains, yet she knew that the best way to handle all pains tossed at her was to accept whatever, all without any excessive cries. She was a heroine to everyone but herself.

As a distraction, Rich would regale her, on those particularly hurting moments, with tales of the days in his youth when Tim was born and the constant bickering that prevailed in that household. Comparing those days to today's life always brought smiles to his face and endless laughter from Val and Tim.

Fortunately, Rich was at home when Val loudly announced that the time had come to, in her words, "Get My Ass to the Hospital." Within seconds, Tim had the bag so labeled in hand. Rich grabbed the keys to his car and the case that had been deemed 'Hospital.' Rich placed Val in a warm jacket and carried her out stairs. Within four minutes, the car was making its final turn on the road that would take then to the hospital,

By the time Rich had parked the car and sped back to the hospital, he arrived at Val's bedside moments after the first signs of a successful delivery had begun. He did manage to grab Val's hand and squeeze it as tightly as he could, but he couldn't get one word out to her. She, on the other hand, didn't even know if anyone was in the room with her.

All in the room began to scream with delight when a little thing began to push its way out of Val. The thing emerging brought with it a series of most impressive cries as it greeted the world.

Dr. Schiff was the first to shout back to the child with a smiling, "Welcome home, you sweet little girl."

It was minutes later that a second baby appeared and even though it looked just like the baby that had preceded it, there was no doubt but that this second arrival was of the masculine breed.

Chapter Sixty-Eight

There was but one argument the three could not resolve. Trying to find the right name for the right child yielded many discussions but not a one they could agree on.

"You two are sure picky. You've turned down some great names I've come up with. Well, here are two more winners. If you don't like them I'm dropping out of this naming game. The boy's name must be 'La Bron' and the perfect girl's name is 'Madonna.'"

Tim stepped back with a big smile awaiting their approval.

"Right on, buddy, they are great names but there is a problem. Their managers would demand a ton of money which we can't afford. Why don't we just let Val pick out the boy's name, and Tim and I could pick out the girl's name?

Val, nodding her head jumped to her feet saying "Right on. And the name for our little man should be 'Tony!'"

Tim immediately shouted his agreement. "And that could force the real Tony to come home and meet our little Tony."

Rich jumped in with, "Great name for the boy and here's a girl's name that's equally perfect. Let's take the name now used by their much loved Grandmother and pass it on to her new granddaughter. Which gives us two equally beautiful ladies named 'Melissa.'"

There were three faces in the room aglow knowing they had solved what could have been a problem, and two blank faces that seemed content with whatever they would be called.

Chapter Sixty-Nine

They were called twins by all; but, truth be told, the boy looked more like their Grandmother and his sister looked more like their Father.

Yes, there was similarity between their faces, their heights and the tone in their voices, but the boy would always listen to what someone else had to say, whereas the girl very rarely would give credence to anyone's opinion but her own. Much like their Father and Mother.

At the young age of fourteen, they had shown great delight in having fun particularly when the fun was at the expense of his or her sister or brother. However, should the animosity be unfairly directed at the female or the male by a non-family enemy, said attacker was directly warned for the trouble they would soon be facing.

Bitter warfare was tolerated when there was only the two of them in the battle. Let there be an outsider in the battle, said warrior would have to face two ruthless allies full force against that "stupid kid."

They competed ruthlessly against one another in almost everything. That was more than true when it came to getting better grades or seeming to be the brighter one. But their love for their parents and for their Uncle Tim was unparalleled. When queried about who was their very best friend they would quickly reply "Uncle Tim is the best friend we could ever have."

It should be noted that Tim's worship of the Twins began at their birth and never ceased.

Dad was known throughout the country as a most talented actor. As a consequence he was regularly approached to perform in theatres throughout the country.

Yes, he worked mostly in Ashland, the family home, but at times a role came his way that could not be ignored. It was both a creative challenge and paid so much money that it could not be turned down.

Both kids nicknamed him their 'part-time Dad' and told everyone that Tim was their real father. Indeed the Twins would spend much time with Tim if Val had gone off with their Dad. Should such an offer come forth in the summer, the entire family would move to that city for much of its run.

Val had happily abandoned any thoughts of acting and dove headlong into writing. Her first novel was of course about a young actress. A small publisher did pick it up and, to their delight, the book received some acclaim.

To say the least it had confirmed to her that she was more a writer than an actress, and she dove full time into writing. Each of her following books received enough acclaim to warrant writing the next book, and on and on and on.

One evening the entire family was stuffing down a meal and speaking away at headlong speed.

Per usual, it was Tim who summed up exactly what was happening. He stood up, clapped his hands and strongly noted, "You are making so much noise that I can't follow what we are talking about."

He then looked at the four others in the room and very softly pronounced "We don't need all that chatter in this family. We know there's only one thing that means anything to us. So, let's all repeat what that is."

With that the entire family shouted as one.
"LOVE MATTERS."